TRAITOR'S ARROW

The Medieval Saga Series
Book Two

David Field

SAPERE
BOOKS

TRAITOR'S ARROW

Published by Sapere Books.

20 Windermere Drive, Leeds, England, LS17 7UZ,
United Kingdom

saperebooks.com

ISBN: 978-1-80055-617-1

PART I

PROLOGUE

The five huntsmen who made up the party slipped furtively from one patch of shade to another as the evening sun launched golden shafts between the oak, ash and elm trees that seemed to go forever. They were moving through that dense portion of the New Forest that surrounded the king's traditional hunting lodge at Brockenhurst. William and Walter crept off to the right, their bows gripped firmly in their left hands, and their arrows neatly quivered over their shoulders for swift access should a stag come into view. Henry, along with the brothers Gilbert and Roger, took the obvious path to the left, doubling over in order to reduce their visibility and squinting into the sun as it descended over distant Ringwood.

William and Walter halted simultaneously as they heard the tell-tale rustle of a deer breaking cover ahead of them to their left. William quickly loaded his bow, and as the startled beast ran past his line of sight, he loosed the shaft. The beast seemed to freeze for a moment, then it let out a hoarse scream and continued running with William's arrow buried in its rump. William shaded his eyes and hastened after it, breaking cover into a patch of bright sunlight. There was the whisper of another discharged arrow, and William stopped abruptly, looking down disbelievingly at his chest. With his free hand he pulled hard at the arrow shaft, but it snapped because, in his shocked state, he had not pulled straight. With a gurgling hiss he fell face forward onto the forest floor, and the tip of the arrow embedded itself even further into his left lung.

Walter gave a cry of horror and raced to William's side, turning his prostrate form over with his boot. Bloody bubbles were already creating a sickening pool on William's green tunic, and Walter stared at it as the others raced over to join him, alerted to the incident by his shouts of disbelief. The brothers Gilbert and Roger were the first into the clearing, and it was the older of the two, Gilbert, who reached down and examined the prostrate form more carefully. Then he looked up at Henry, who was the last to reach the body of William.

'Your brother is no more, Henry. Ride hard to Winchester before his death is more widely broadcast, seize the Treasury and make good your claim. We will see to the removal of the body.'

Henry looked blankly at the brothers, stunned by what had just happened, and the advice he was being given. Then he looked enquiringly at Walter, who shook his head vigorously.

'It was not I! The fatal shaft came from over there,' he added, nodding towards the area of the forest from which the remainder had raced upon hearing Walter's cries. Then Gilbert walked a few paces to his left and picked up the broken-off shaft, with its distinctive feather.

'There were but six such shafts handed to William ere we set out,' he reminded Walter. 'They were the fletcher's finest, and they were a gift for William. But he gave two to you, and you have only one left in your quiver.'

'I loosed the first one at that boar we encountered earlier,' Walter explained in his own defence, but the remainder of the party continued to stare at him accusingly. He backed slowly away from them, and just before he turned to run, Gilbert offered some advice.

'If you run now, we'll delay removing the body, or telling anyone what has happened. The coast is but an hour away by fast horse — you may be in Normandy before William's body reaches Winchester. Fly — now!'

Walter took off through the leaf litter, leaping over protruding tree roots and around clumps of gorse in his haste to escape. His horse had been tied to a tree further back towards the hunting lodge they had left an hour earlier, and he untied it, leapt into the saddle and thundered off towards Lymington. He was followed, shortly thereafter, by Henry, who lost no time in galloping to Winchester, and the future that had suddenly opened up before him.

Gilbert looked across at his brother Roger and smiled. 'Will you take the head or the feet?'

'Neither,' Roger grinned back. 'Henry needs time to reach Winchester, and Walter must be allowed to make good his escape to France. If we leave the bastard here, the foresters may not find him until the boars and foxes have taken their share. By then, we could both be in London, where we might be safer lodged.'

Gilbert was hardly likely to object to this proposal. After all, the man whose body they were abandoning had been, for the past thirteen years, King of England.

I

1074

Sir Wilfrid de Walsingham smiled proudly as his oldest child, Matilda, waved to him from the doorway of the shrine from which she had just emerged, holding the hand of her aunt Elva. Matilda still called her 'Aunt Elva', since she was her father's sister, but everyone else was required to call her 'Sister Grace', since she was now in holy orders in The Convent of the Holy Sisters of the Blessed Virgin. Even her brother Sir Wilfrid had agreed to address her by the name under which she had been called to God's work, in return for her not lowering the dignity of the lord of the manor by calling him 'Will'. This was the name by which he had been known when they had grown up together in the village of Sandlake — over a week's journey away on the south coast near Pevensey, in the old Earldom of Wessex, as it had been called then.

'The Holy Lady requires another coat of paint,' Matilda shouted up to him. 'Could you ask Ralph Builder to make sure that the gold doesn't flake off this time?'

'And who is to pay for that?' her father enquired teasingly, but it was his sister, as usual, who had the glib answer she gave to almost every question to do with the shrine.

'God will provide. And if He doesn't, the rents are due in at Martinmas, and it's been a good harvest. Since the good Lord has been so benevolent towards His people, the least they can do is pay an extra penny each, in order to see His mother's statue restored to its former beauty.'

Wilfrid waved in acknowledgment of her faith, if not her commercial wisdom, and marvelled again at the swift conversion that had transformed Elva from the spirited creature who had delighted in racing him up and down the path beside the river back in Sandlake. This was where their father's mill had ground the thegn's grain, in the days before William of Normandy's warships had appeared on the coastline below their humble village. Elva had been married to the thegn's second son Selwyn, whose grave she tended daily in her holy vestments. It was only yards away from the shrine itself, down the slope towards the river where Wilfrid had recently installed a mill of his own, for the benefit of his tenants and cottars.

Between childhood and widowhood, Elva had borne a child, a boy called Elston who was barely a year younger than Matilda, or 'Tilly' as she was known within the family circle. Elston had been absorbed into Wilfrid's household when Elva had taken the veil after her husband's death. Selwyn's body had been brought back to Walsingham draped across his horse, and Elva had, in her own mind, finally received the sign for which she had prayed to the Virgin, asking whether or not her life should be devoted to the service of God.

Neither Wilfrid nor Elva had received any Christian education, if one discounted the mumbles of the passing friars who told unlikely stories in return for food and drink. However, from the moment they had been directed to Walsingham by their benefactor, Earl Waltheof of Huntingdon, Elva had been overcome by something that had drawn her daily to the statue of the Virgin Mary that was housed inside the shrine. It had previously been under the sole patronage of the former Lady Richeldis de Faverches, who was now happy to be known as 'Mother Magdalena', the head of the convent she had founded.

The Holy Mother would insist, to anyone who was prepared to listen, that the shrine had been created by the Virgin herself, overnight, following her visitation upon the former Richeldis. Whether it was true or not, the shrine was rapidly attracting more and more pilgrims, and the primary work of the order of nuns that Richeldis had founded was the preservation of the shrine and the daily offertories made while prostrated before the Virgin's statue.

Wilfrid himself was almost prepared to believe that there was something magical about the place. It had been where both families had sought sanctuary during the wave of slaughter that had marked King William's suppression of the early rebellions against his rule in the days following the battle fought on Senlac Ridge, immediately above the village that the former Will and Elva Riveracre had grown up in. This had been the battle in which Wilfrid and Selwyn had fought shoulder to shoulder to defend the old Saxon way of life under the ultimate command of the former King Harold Godwinson. They had lost, but had remained alive through the intercession of a Norman monk. The monk had had cause to be grateful to the villagers, who had protected him from King Harold, and he had proved to be the Conqueror's former chaplain.

Both Wilfrid and Selwyn had been fleeing the Conqueror's wrath, following their separate desertions from his service as he added reluctant Saxons to his retinue, when they'd been befriended by Waltheof, then Earl of Huntingdon. He'd recruited them to guard the Virgin's shrine and Lady Richeldis. Not that Waltheof himself was religious — his reason for wishing the Lady Richeldis to be guarded had more to do with her own prior existence, as Edith Swan Neck, the widow of the late King Harold. Until Saxon resentment was entirely eliminated from this still volatile nation, she would remain a rallying point for those who had no love for their new Norman overlords, even though she might now be draped in holy vestments.

It was in defence of this beautiful sanctuary that Wilfrid and Selwyn had taken part in the successful campaign by Waltheof against the brigand Hereward, who had posed a threat to its peaceful existence. Selwyn had been killed by Hereward's hand, and Wilfrid had been knighted and granted his estate by King William, who had believed that he'd been battling Hereward to defend his master's ill-gotten throne. Still, it was an ill wind, as the saying went, and now Wilfrid was elevated to a status far higher than a simple Saxon miller's son could ever have contemplated.

But it came at a considerable price. King William had brought over with him a new system of government. It proceeded from a concept novel to Saxon ears, namely that the entire nation belonged to the monarch, who then leased it out to his leading nobles in return for their servitude, and in particular their service to him in battle. These leading nobles, in turn, sub-leased the massive estates they had been granted to lesser men — knights such as Wilfrid, who owed their continued livelihood to the higher nobles, in return for supplying the armed retinues that their feudal overlords were bonded to muster under the royal banner.

By this simple arrangement, in theory, the king had everyone bound to him in military service, and even the lord of a modest manor such as Walsingham was required to keep a standing army of sorts, recruited from his own tenants and cottars. This system of government was alien to what had gone before, when men were called to a Saxon earl's "fyrd", a temporary army raised only in times of national or regional crisis. The ad hoc "fyrd" system had proved ineffective against the more permanent armed aggression of a standing army such as King William had brought across the narrow strip of water from northern France. Now, the Saxons were a conquered race, either burning with resentment or silent in their indifference or fear.

Almost ten years ago, Wilfrid had thrown in his hand with the invader in the hope of preserving the lives of his fellow Saxons, who had no idea just how powerful and ruthless their new king could be when faced with resistance. Now Wilfrid was one of the few lords of the manor whose birthright was Saxon, and he could just see beyond the current chaos towards a more peaceful and well-regulated future.

Wilfrid walked back into the manor house that had once belonged to Mother Magdalena. He smiled as his eyes lit upon the now slightly rounded figure of his wife Joan, as she bustled and fussed around their two housemaids, Wendel and Martha, while they laid out the bread slices that would serve as trenchers for the roast fowl and fish from the estate. Joan had once been a serving girl herself, but in the Court of King Edward the Confessor, where Wilfrid had met her when he was recruited as a royal housecarl. She had been fresh-faced and flaxen-haired in those days, and there were still traces of her former colouring, mixed with the grey streaks crammed down under her functional cap. But her body had filled out after giving birth, first to Matilda, then to her younger brother Thomas, who was now an eight-year-old with boundless energy that Wilfrid could only envy. Thomas was following the serving girls up and down the table, with a broom between his legs as a make-believe horse.

'Leave that to Wendel and Martha, my sweet,' Wilfrid urged Joan as he walked over, placed his arm around her waist and kissed her on the cheek. She was glistening with sweat as the fire in the hearth began to consume the pine logs that their steward Edgar had piled in there an hour earlier, in defence against the early autumn winds that could turn into a howling gale in minutes.

'Everything must be right for the entertainment of such an important visitor,' Joan insisted, as she tried to bat Thomas's ear when he hopped past her on his imaginary steed. 'Thomas, if you don't get out of my way, I'll use that broom on your backside! Now, go out and play with Elston or something.'

'Elston won't play with me,' Thomas grumbled, 'ever since I climbed the great meadow oak faster than him. And Tilly just wants to play girlish games with her dolls.'

'Outside, Thomas — now!' Wilfrid ordered.

Thomas hopped outside after instructing his broom to proceed: 'Full gallop — engage the enemy.'

'God forbid that he's ever called upon to do that on a real horse,' Wilfrid muttered as his gaze followed his son's ungainly departure through the hall door. 'And I hope that's not why the Justiciar is visiting us.'

Indeed, it was a rare event for the Chief Justiciar of England, Richard Fitz Gilbert, to be descending upon a humble manor in Norfolk, but he was known to have made the same visitations to Stowmarket and Framlingham. He had spent the previous night in Swaffham, and Walsingham was the next manor on what was obviously a planned progress. Wilfrid and Joan were familiar enough with the twice-yearly inspections from their immediate overlord Ralph de Gael, Earl of Norfolk, but their impending new visitor, as Chief Justiciar of England, was one of three men who had been left in charge of England while King William saw to his interests in Normandy, where he had been for over a year now, with no reported English uprisings in his absence.

The sun was setting over distant Norwich when the small retinue trotted through the front gate under the banner of red chevrons on a yellow background that constituted the family crest of the Fitz Gilberts. The men at arms were to be billeted in the old barracks that had once housed Wilfrid's standing force of twenty or so. He strode out with Joan and the family to effect the welcome and the introductions.

'The lovely young lady presenting you with her entire doll collection is my daughter Matilda,' Wilfrid smiled up at Fitz Gilbert, 'and the small boy eyeing your horse is my son Thomas. There is another boy called Elston, who is probably in hiding in case he's done something naughty, and you are his punishment. My wife Joan and I are both happy and humbled to be providing you with our modest hospitality.'

Fitz Gilbert grinned as he dismounted and shook Wilfrid's hand. 'I have a house full of my own, when I am free to visit it, which is not often in these troubled times.'

'Troubled?'

'Let us go inside, and I may then disclose why I am here.'

A short while later, Wilfrid listened with sadness and a sense of foreboding to what Richard Fitz Gilbert had to impart.

'King William grows over-confident of the loyalty of his barons — even those who, like myself and my co-regent William de Warenne, came over here as part of the original invasion. I am advised that you were there too.'

Wilfrid grimaced with embarrassment. 'I was, but on *top* of the ridge.'

Richard smiled back reassuringly. 'I would have been both surprised and disappointed had you said anything else. You were clearly defending your king, as would any loyal subject, and I am advised that you now do so in respect of our current king, even though he is mostly in Normandy these days.'

'Of course,' Wilfrid assured him. 'I owe him all this,' he added with a gesture that acknowledged the hall in which they were seated.

'Well, it is that loyalty that our king must rely on in the coming weeks,' Richard announced.

Wilfrid's face fell. 'We are being invaded?'

'Not yet, but that may be part of their overall plan.'

'Whose?'

'I get ahead of myself,' Richard replied as he took another sip of wine. 'As I already mentioned, King William deemed the time appropriate to return to Normandy, where he is somewhat distracted by the actions of his neighbours in Maine and the Vexin. He has been thus engaged for some time, and in his absence certain ungrateful nobles here in England who owe him everything have seen fit to stage a rebellion.'

'We have heard nothing of this here,' Wilfrid advised him with a frown.

'It has mainly been in Hereford,' Richard disclosed, 'since one of the leaders is its earl, Roger de Breteuil. But he is in league with your own immediate overlord, the Earl of Norfolk, Ralph de Gael, and it may be that you will be called to his service in the normal way. I am here to warn you against it, since to serve de Gael at this time would be deemed an act of treason.'

'So if the earl calls out my small retinue, I must refuse?' Wilfrid enquired, as Joan slipped her hand nervously under his arm and grasped his elbow, given that her rudimentary French was sufficient for her to follow the general nature of what was being discussed.

'Indeed you must, and I will of course report your loyalty to King William upon his return, whenever that might be.'

'He is not returning in person to quell the uprising?'

'He does not consider it to be sufficiently serious, following my advice. But your old loyalties may be tested in another way.'

'How?'

'You first came here at the invitation of Earl Waltheof, did you not, when he was Earl of Huntingdon?'

'Indeed we did, and we shall be forever grateful to him for that.'

'That is my concern,' Richard frowned. 'He is said to have joined the rebels in a bid for the throne.'

Wilfrid took this information in, then shook his head sadly. 'He is not only unwise, but also ungrateful. He is the only remaining Saxon to retain an earldom, since Edwin and Morcar were done to death following the northern uprisings. He was also pardoned for his support of a Danish invasion that was planned for the same time, and he received further royal favour when he was created Earl of Northumbria, and allowed to marry William's niece — Judith, I believe her name is. Why, now, should he be rebelling?'

Richard grinned. 'Without wishing to appear ungallant, you have clearly not seen the Countess Judith. And neither has Waltheof for some time, or so it is rumoured. Theirs is hardly a love match.'

'But when King William hears of this, he will surely take his head clean from his shoulders, after so many past forgivenesses?'

'He already knows, and his rage was reported to be dreadful to behold. It is only a matter of time before this rebellion is suppressed, but I have need of you and your men on the coast.'

'For what, precisely?' Wilfrid enquired.

'To guard it against possible invasion by Canute of Denmark. He has been waiting for some time to pursue what he believes to be his ancestral right to the English throne, and it is believed that he has been invited by Ralph de Gael to invade. Since Ralph's lands are here in Norfolk, if Canute invades he will likely regard any men at arms he sees on the coastline to be welcoming him onto our shores. By the time he learns of his mistake, your men will have put *his* men to the sword.'

'I hope that he comes before next year's harvest,' Wilfrid grimaced as Joan leaned into him.

Richard eyed him sternly. 'You have disbanded your force?'

'Yes and no. Those men who lived after putting Hereward to flight have settled here, and most of them are farming on my manor in return for armed service when required. But the needs of the estate are such that they can only be spared from tilling their crops, tending their animals, and following their trades as builders, fleshers, blacksmiths and the like for one day a week. That is tomorrow, as it transpires, so you may watch them drilling, should you so wish.'

Richard shook his head. 'Tomorrow I must return to my lands in Suffolk, ahead of laying siege to Norwich. I would have commanded you and your men to join me in that, but you are closer to the coast, and so I leave its defences in your hands.'

II

For the next two months, Wilfrid deployed his converted farmers, builders and field labourers along the sand dunes and shingle beaches of North Norfolk, their eyes permanently on the North Sea horizon for sight of Danish sails. Wilfrid was able to use up the time, and the men's energy, in military exercise and weapons training, to the point at which he had every confidence that should the Danes dare to come ashore, a sizeable number of them would end their days face-down on it. But given that the band under his command never once rose to more than thirty in number, Wilfrid also realised that if there were to be an invasion, he would be leading what amounted to a suicidal delaying action. More than once he asked himself if it was all worth it, and in his darkest hours he wished that he had remained in Sandlake to inherit his father's mill.

Unknown to Wilfrid and his men, any prospect of rebellion in the land immediately behind them had fizzled out quickly, when Waltheof was betrayed by his far from loving wife Judith. Waltheof was forced to make a confession to Lanfranc, King William's loyal Archbishop of Canterbury. The same clergyman brought Roger de Breteuil, Earl of Hereford, and his followers to heel by excommunicating all of them, while Ralph de Gael left his stronghold of Norwich Castle under the guardianship of his wife and fled back to his native Brittany. Richard Fitz Gilbert's forces put Norwich under siege until the countess surrendered, and was allowed to join her husband in Brittany bearing the not unexpected news that he was no longer Earl of Norfolk.

The Danes finally appeared on the horizon long after the internal rebellion had been put down. But they somehow learned that there would be no reinforcements awaiting them in Norfolk, and instead sailed further north, to their traditional hunting ground of York, which they harassed for a few days before burning and pillaging their way back to their waiting vessels. They had received news that King William was finally back in England, and he was heading their way with an army that grew larger the further north it marched. By the time the king reached York, it was empty of Danes, but still full of Yorkshiremen who would gladly have hauled him from his warhorse and slit his throat after what he had done to their countryside only five years previously, in the so-called 'harrowing of the north'.

King William therefore deemed it appropriate to return south, where he celebrated the Christmas of 1075 at Winchester, still regarded as the centre of government, as it had once been under the Earls of Wessex, except now it was the government of all of England. Wilfrid and his defending force were relieved of their duties in the sand dunes around Cromer five weeks prior to Christmas, and Richard Fitz Gilbert advised Wilfrid that he was invited to Court to be thanked personally by King William.

Joan pouted, as her husband knew she would, when she assumed that after two months away Wilfrid was planning to journey south, leaving her once again as a single parent of three children — only two of whom were her own — in the depths of yet another freezing Norfolk winter.

Wilfrid smiled and took both her hands in his. 'I was not told that you could not accompany me, and we can visit Sandlake once again, either on the way there or the way back.'

'But what about the children?'

'They will be safe enough with Elva and Richeldis, and we have done more than our share of acting as second parents to Richeldis's son Geoffrey on days when her holy duties keep her confined inside the shrine. If the weather holds, we should not be gone beyond a month, and you can once again experience life inside a royal court.'

Joan grimaced. 'The first time was enough for me, and at least I spoke the language. All I hear from the king's nobles who visit us is French.'

'What better chance to learn some more, then? And surely you wish to see Sandlake again? It was where Matilda was born, remember?'

'I'm hardly likely to forget,' Joan replied. 'But if it's what you wish, then of course I'll come with you.'

Winchester was barely recognisable from the last time that Wilfrid had seen it. There was now a stone keep in its centre, with a massive defensive tower, on the ground floor of which was a temporary hall while plans were being laid for a new Great Hall in a separate building. King William was in a generous mood, and having left his queen, Matilda, behind to manage his estates in Normandy, he had brought some of their extensive brood of children with him, to celebrate their first Christmas in England. They were all boys, and sharply contrasted in their appearance and personalities.

The oldest was now a man, although he was so short that only his stubbly dark beard confirmed that he was out of childhood. His name was Robert, and his next youngest brother, another William, seemed to take great delight in provoking or embarrassing him by calling him by what was presumably his nickname of 'Curthose', a polite version of 'short arse'. This middle son, William, was already displaying signs of a dissolute temperament and a wayward nature —

frequently imbibing too much wine and swearing loudly at serving staff, openly blaspheming even in the presence of clergymen, and picking fights with court nobles who were too terrified of causing him serious injury to be able to fight back.

He was altogether an unpleasant youth of some fifteen years of age, and easily distinguished among the courtly throng, even at a distance, by reason of his flaming red hair, which had begun to earn him the nickname of 'Rufus', only ever used when he was out of earshot. The third, and youngest, of the boys, was little more than an infant: a small, quiet, studious little barrel called Henry. He was approximately eight years of age, so far as Wilfrid could make out, and it occurred to him that Henry may well have been the child that Queen Matilda had been carrying in her womb during the progress from Tamworth to York. Wilfrid had been part of the escort, performing translation duties for King William who even now steadfastly refused to speak English.

When Wilfrid and Joan finally arrived at Winchester in an early winter blizzard, and were shown to their accommodation in a recently completed building just inside the main keep, they discovered that the court was in mourning for yet another royal prince, the second-born Richard, who had only reached seventeen years of age. He had lost his life in some sort of hunting accident in the nearby New Forest.

The more superstitious of those to whom Wilfrid spoke — Saxons who were only too happy to converse in English — claimed that Richard's death was the outcome of a curse laid on the forest, which had been brutally cleared of families that had lived and worked there for generations in order to make more room for deer that King William delighted in slaughtering. To add to the insult and injustice, anyone caught either killing the deer, or even cutting down the greenery on which they grazed, would either be hanged or roasted upside down on a hastily constructed spit to discourage their family and neighbours.

Since the proclaimed period of mourning did not expire for another three days, Wilfrid and Joan took the opportunity to slip away from court and head back down the road towards London, before branching down the well-worn track that led to the shoreline at Pevensey. Wilfrid in particular was apprehensive about what sort of welcome they might receive. When the couple had taken their leave eight years previously, it had been down an avenue of cheering locals who had finally acknowledged that 'Will', as they knew him, had been working for their benefit rather than for his own. However, he was now returning as 'Sir Wilfrid', with a manor estate of his own granted to him by the conquering monarch whose army had slaughtered some of Sandlake's finest young men.

Nothing appeared to be greatly changed as they eased their horses down the Powdermill track towards the mill, whose huge centre wheel was sitting motionless in its cradle. Given the harsh weather of recent days, this was perhaps to be expected. They turned in between the rows of huts, seemingly unchanged in their absence, until they reached the one in which Will had been raised. With a welcoming shout of warning he pulled back the door covering, and they stepped inside.

Seated by the fire, covered in what looked like sheep hides, was a wizened old man who Will recognised instantly as his father, Eldred. He strode the few feet towards the fire with outstretched arms.

'Father!' he called, then stopped as the old man looked up with unseeing eyes.

'Is that young Will?' Eldred croaked.

A slight figure slipped from the corner into full view. She was a woman in her early forties, by the look of her, with straight grey hair and a pinched, unfed look. Her eyes glinted for a moment as she recognised the visitor, then she explained. 'I'm afraid yer dad lost his sight with this latest bout of whatever keeps ailing him. They reckon this one'll be his last, so there's perhaps a blessing of sorts.'

'My mother?' Will croaked as the tears began to well inside him.

'Gone two years back, with the ague that took a lot o' the older folk, including old Thegn Leofric. I only just escaped it myself. Don't yer recognise me anymore, Will Riveracre? It's Annis, and my man Deman works the mill for yer old dad.'

Will stared at her. In her younger days as a thrall girl, Annis had been the focus of all his pubescent fantasies, which she had rejected. She had then attained her own hut and planting strip by becoming involved with the thegn's older son, who had died in the battle on Senlac Ridge. After that, she'd hooked one of the strongest men in Sandlake, Will's old boyhood enemy Deman Flesher, who had become his firm friend when together they'd reformed the old village fyrd, apprehensive that Duke William might revisit the village in revenge.

'He's "Sir Wilfrid de Walsingham" now,' Joan chipped in proudly, aware of their history.

'That don't cut no barley around here,' Annis replied. 'He's still "Will Riveracre" when he comes back ter where he belongs.'

'That's my boy yer talkin' about,' Eldred chirped up from beside the fire. 'Tell his mam ter get the mead out ter welcome him home. An' where's Elva taken herself off to? She should be helpin' her mam cook the supper.'

Will looked enquiringly across at Annis, who dropped her gaze.

'I'm afraid his eyesight ain't the only thing that's goin', Will,' she said.

Will gave a choking sob and threw himself onto his knees, gripping his father to him in a massive hug as his shoulders shook with grief. Joan shuffled forward to stand next to him, a comforting hand on his shoulder. After ten minutes or so he stood up, wiped the tears from his face, and untied the soft bag that hung from his waist. He held it out for Annis, who took it from him with muttered thanks.

'It's not much, Annis, but it's all I brought with me. I hadn't expected to find this.'

'And we hadn't expected to see you ever again,' Annis replied quietly.

'And you won't — not ever again. Come on, Joan.'

They slipped sadly out of the hut, and Will looked back one more time before they untied their horses. He helped Joan into the saddle.

'That was the life I once led. I spent over twenty years as a Saxon, ten of them trying to save Saxons from Normans — or was it from themselves? Either way, the future lies up the track there. We're Normans now, whether we like it or not.'

III

Two days after the somewhat subdued Christmas celebrations, each of the invitees had been summoned to meet individually with the king. Aware that he was the first on the list, Wilfrid rose early, washed, put on his best tunic and hose, and made his way towards the temporary hall through the noise of masons recommencing work on the new Great Hall across the keep. Because of the outside noise, Wilfrid was not aware, until he tentatively pushed open the heavy wooden door, that there was anything going on inside. But what met his eyes was the last thing he had expected to see.

The king had not yet arrived, but two of his sons obviously had, although whether the younger of the two was there voluntarily was far from clear. The older boy by at least eight years, the ruddy-faced and red-haired William, was pinning his squealing and protesting little brother Henry to the floor with one arm across his neck.

Without thinking — and with the same instinctive actions that he had regularly been obliged to employ in order to separate his own son Thomas and his nephew Elston — Wilfrid raced over to the corner in which the two boys were struggling, and pulled William 'Rufus' to his feet by the scruff of his tunic neck and the seat of his hose. Rufus swore and blasphemed, revealing an impressive repertoire of oaths for a boy of his age, as he kicked and struggled, but Wilfrid hung on tightly. Henry wriggled free, stood up, and gave a sneer as his older brother was cuffed across the ear by this tall, lanky saviour who had appeared from nowhere.

Rufus finally ceased blaspheming and found a more coherent theme. 'When I am king, you will pay for that with your head!'

'*If* you ever get to be king, I shall make it my business to depart the nation,' Wilfrid yelled back, 'for it deserves better than to be ruled by a bully like you! If your own brother is not safe from your wicked actions, what chance have the rest of us?'

Rufus was about to reply with something suitably obscene when his jaw suddenly dropped, and his eyes opened wide in fear as he gazed over Wilfrid's shoulder. Wilfrid looked round quickly, instinctively reaching for the dagger that always hung from his belt. Then he let his hand drop back to his side, since threatening a king was presumably not a wise thing to do.

King William chuckled quietly to himself, then glared at Rufus. 'Go to your chamber immediately, and see to your learning! Your tutor is not pleased with your progress, and there are better ways of conducting yourself before those who will one day be your subjects. Go — now!'

Rufus scuttled away with a final menacing glare at Wilfrid, and Henry dusted himself down, adjusted his hose one final time, and slinked away, shamefaced.

The king beckoned for Wilfrid to join him on the bench near the window. 'Do you understand boys?'

'I like to think so,' Wilfrid smiled back, 'since I have two of my own. Strictly speaking I have one of my own, but I also look after my sister's boy, who is now fatherless after our sally against Hereward in the Fens.'

The king nodded. 'I thought I recognised your face, and now I remember. I knighted you on that occasion, did I not?'

'You did indeed, sire.'

'Is that why I invited you to spend Christmas here, because you put paid to Hereward?'

'That was some time ago, sire. I believe that the reason for your generous invitation was the result of my men guarding your Norfolk shore against a threatened Danish invasion.'

'Yes — that was it, of course. Fitz Gilbert told me of your loyalty and bravery. But I also seem to recall that we had earlier dealings — not long after I invaded?'

Wilfrid swallowed hard, and hoped that his desertion from previous royal service would not be remembered, as he explained. 'During your first few months — before and during your coronation — I assisted in translating from French for the benefit of those of my people who could not understand that you came in peace.'

'Yes, and although your French is now excellent, it was unfortunate that so many of your people had to learn the hard way that I was not here simply for a holiday. Though I must admit, you acquit yourself well for a Saxon — more like a Norman.'

'Thank you, sire. I shall regard that as a compliment.'

'As indeed you should. You are from Norfolk, did you say?'

'Yes, sire.'

'So who is your liege lord, since de Gael was stripped of Norwich following his escape to Brittany?'

'I have no idea, sire. Before him it was Waltheof, but he became Earl of Northumbria.'

'He will also become a corpse ere I leave England again,' the king muttered as he spat into the rushes. 'So you have no liege lord? To whom do you propose to answer the summons, should we have further need of your services?'

'Perhaps the Justiciar Fitz Gilbert, since it was his summons that I last answered?'

'Yes, that would seem to be appropriate, since he holds lands in Clare, which I believe is in Suffolk. Is that close to Norfolk?'

'Just to the south, sire.'

'Very well, then — answer to him. But that reminds me that we need a new Earl of East Anglia, or Norwich, or wherever. Might you be prepared to accept such a title?'

'In the fullness of time, I would of course be delighted to serve Your Majesty in such a role. But I feel that I must first further prove my prowess in battle. It has been some time now, I fear.'

'Very well. At least I need not fear your ambition. You may leave me now, but ask the steward to bring me some wine, if you would be so good.'

They rode home over tracks hard with frost, to discover that in their absence there had been a minor crisis. Flushed by his triumph in climbing the old oak at the foot of the river meadow quicker than his cousin Elston, Thomas had issued a similar challenge to Geoffrey, Mother Magdalena's son by the former King Harold, whose widow she was. Geoffrey had, by force of necessity, grown up almost as part of Wilfrid's household, and he was now a robust youth of ten, almost two years older than Thomas and obviously gifted with his father's stubborn and determined temperament. He had eagerly accepted the challenge from his more willowy childhood companion, and had been in one of the topmost branches of the now rotting remnant of a cleared patch of forest when it had snapped, taking Geoffrey with it to the ground, from which he had proved unable to rise. In his fall, he had dislodged other weakened branches, one of which had struck

Thomas a direct blow to the side of his head, laying him out cold.

Had the entire incident not been witnessed, the two boys might have lain there much longer, but aid was summoned without delay, and the two boys had been lowered onto adjoining pallets inside Thomas's chamber in the manor house, where they had been prayed over by Geoffrey's mother and Thomas's aunt until the arrival of Merrys Winterborn, the local midwife and 'wise woman'. A brief argument had ensured between the middle-aged nun, who believed that everything should be left to God, and the village matron, who knew better. Magdalena had reluctantly allowed Merrys to secure Geoffrey's leg with two planks of wood cut from the straighter branches of a nearby elm, while Thomas was revived by waving under his nose the fumes from a burning bowl of plants whose precise origin Merrys refused to disclose.

Sister Grace lost no time in recounting the entire business to Wilfrid and Joan on their return to Walsingham, and they hurried into the room where both boys were still lying, under daily threats from Mother Magdalena of dire consequences if they moved. Joan threw her arms around her son, Thomas, and enquired as to how he was feeling.

'I'm fine, Mother, and I have been since the day after it happened. Elston keeps coming in here to gloat, because he can play outside and I'm not allowed. *Please* make Tilly stop coming in here to insist that her dolls tell me stories.'

'You're both lucky to be alive,' Wilfrid advised him. 'Stop feeling so sorry for yourself, when poor Geoffrey here is likely to be confined indoors with his broken leg for a lot longer than you. What possessed the pair of you to venture up that rickety old oak, when everyone knew that it was ready to fall down?'

'It was a challenge,' Geoffrey replied from the other cot, as if this was all that was required to justify his actions. 'A true knight never backs away from a challenge.'

'You're not a knight,' Wilfrid reminded him.

'I will be one day, just like you,' Geoffrey insisted, 'and when I am, I'll take Thomas and Elston with me as my squires. That's all they're good for.'

Wilfrid knelt by Geoffrey's pallet, and looked sternly into his eyes. 'I'm not your father, so I can't tell you what to do, but there is no way on this earth that you're taking Thomas — who *is* my son — or Elston, who is my nephew, into any sort of armed warfare. I've seen battlefields for myself, and please believe me when I tell you that I never wish to see another one.'

'But you're a brave knight!' Geoffrey countered.

Wilfrid shook his head. 'I'm a *lucky* knight, that's all. Bravery is for idiots with no imagination.'

Geoffrey was back on his feet by the time that spring turned into summer, although he would walk with a limp for the next two harvests, as he proved his impending manhood by taking his place among the estate boys lifting and stacking hay bales. Thomas seemed to heed the example of what had happened to Geoffrey, while Elston developed his growing interest in learning, to the delight of his mother Elva. In her capacity as Sister Grace, she had hopes of opening some sort of school for the children of the estate.

'I do believe that one day Elston might be encouraged to take holy orders himself,' she confided in Joan as they sat shelling peas from the small garden they tended at the side of the manor house.

'I hope he doesn't turn into one of those disgusting priests who used to hang around West Minster Palace, waiting for the chance to touch us as we walked past them,' Joan observed sourly.

Elva chuckled. 'One of our visiting friars did that to me once. I kicked him in the place that, now I'm in holy orders, I cannot name.'

IV

This idyllic way of life continued for the next two years, and Wilfrid was just beginning to reassure himself that he would be able to celebrate his fortieth birthday with all his limbs intact when a messenger clattered in from Richard Fitz Gilbert. Wilfrid enjoyed only the briefest of farewells before he found himself bucketing up and down in a leaky old vessel, heaving and lurching its way down the Channel to Caen, where King William awaited all those who had been summoned. So far as Wilfrid could make out from the few facts within Richard's own knowledge, there was disquiet among the members of the royal family, and one of the sons had broken free of parental control.

Once Wilfrid and the few men who had accompanied him had settled in at the barrack block, and Wilfrid had begun to speak with the armed retainers who 'Duke William' kept permanently based in his Normandy capital, he learned why he had been summoned, along with dozens of other knights and their immediate entourage. He was told, amidst laughter and slighting references to his lack of height, that King William's oldest son Robert had stormed off after becoming the victim of a prank by his younger brothers.

The middle son William had prevailed upon his younger brother Henry, who seemed to live in fear of him, to join him in urinating in a chamber pot. They had then waited until Robert was taking his daily exercise under the castle walls, and had leaned out and poured the entire contents onto his head. Robert was particularly sensitive about his dignity, and was already feeling slighted because of his father's refusal to grant him estates of his own to govern. He therefore took it very badly when his legitimate complaint regarding the behaviour of his younger brothers was met only by a loud guffaw of amusement from their father.

Deeply stung, and feeling further humiliated, he had ridden out of Caen with many of the younger sons of leading Norman nobles who hung around him. They had taken over the castle at Rémalard, a day's ride south of Caen, from which stronghold they had then begun raiding the countryside. It was embarrassing enough for Duke William to have his son rebelling against him in his own dukedom, but the matter was made more serious by the fact that one of Robert's fellow rebels was Roger Fitz Gilbert, the son of Chief Justiciar Richard Fitz Gilbert of England, who had gained so much from King William during his distribution of English honours. It was partly for this reason that Fitz Gilbert had been ordered back to Normandy to chastise his own son while Duke William saw to his. Richard had been ordered to bring over with him 'that knight from Norfolk who defended us against the Danes, and who understands boys.'

Those who had answered the summons to Caen were told to prepare to lay siege to Rémalard. When Wilfrid rode out alongside Fitz Gilbert, and under his banner, Duke William spotted him and ordered that he ride with the royal party. As their two warhorses trotted dutifully alongside each other under their heavy burdens, Duke William, with his English crown proudly atop his battle helm, turned to Wilfrid.

'Do your sons rebel in this manner?'

'No, sire, but neither do they have piss-pots emptied on their heads.'

'I should have chastised both his brothers, I suppose, but Henry is too young to have known any better. As for William,

I have obliged him to ride with us in order to witness the consequences of his actions, and to apologise to his brother when this is over.'

Wilfrid opted to remain silent. From what he had seen of the arrogant and overbearing younger William, apologies were not something that came easily to him, and the duke was blandly assuming that the rebellion would end peacefully.

Robert and his supporters fled Rémalard when advised that Duke William was riding out to suppress the revolt, but at this point King Philip of France saw his opportunity to drive a further wedge between the older and younger generations of the family that held Normandy while refusing to pay him homage for it. He invited the rebels to hold out in the much better fortified castle at Gerberoi, closer to Paris and the disputed area of the Vexin that had been the source of territorial squabbles for many years.

After three weeks, the siege had reached the stage at which one might normally expect those inside Gerberoi to either raise the white flag of surrender, or attempt to break the enemy ring around the town walls by staging a desperate break-out. They chose the latter, and as the rebel forces led by Robert Curthose thundered out through the western gate, those grouped around Duke William, including Sir Wilfrid Walsingham, pulled into a tighter knot and braced for the impact. It came in a deafening clash of steel, the squeal of terrified horses, and the curses of men who had been injured when the front ranks engaged. King William was seeking to hold his restless horse steady, one hand on its bridle and the other brandishing his drawn sword, when one of those who had recently broken out of the town jumped from his horse in full battle armour and ducked under the king's rearing steed.

Wilfrid barely had the chance to recognise that the warrior in question was Robert, before the son had slashed the saddle leathers from the underside of the king's destrier. As the horse reared again in fear, the entire saddle equipage slid from its back, and King William lay on the dusty ground, a cumbersome figure in his full armour, and with the extra body weight that was the legacy of several years of peace. Robert raised his own sword into the vertical position over his father's throat, in the symbolic time-honoured gesture that he had him at his mercy, and could either dispatch him or accept his formal surrender. He then found his own throat pricked sharply by Wilfrid's sword point as he leapt from his own horse to give battle. The two men eyed each other for a moment, and it was Wilfrid who spoke first, raising his voice to be heard amidst the shouts, screams, curses, and clatter of battle.

'That is no way to respect your father, Robert of Normandy. Sheath your sword and salute him in apology, or I will put my own sword through your ungrateful throat. The choice is yours.'

'You would hang!' Robert yelled back.

'I would indeed,' was Wilfrid's reply, 'but you would already be dead.'

After the briefest of staring contests between the two men, Robert sheathed his sword and yelled up at Wilfrid. 'You may both leave the field unharmed, but you — Saxon scum — will one day pay for this with your life!'

Robert turned and raced back through his own lines, calling on his men to keep pushing forward. Behind the king and Wilfrid, it was obvious that the besiegers had lost. Those who had been holding out against them were about to escape, running unmolested through the rear ranks of William's forces that were commanded by William Rufus. Wilfrid grabbed the bridle of his horse, which had, by some miracle, not run off during all the chaos surrounding it, and held it out towards the king.

'Take my horse and flee the field, sire!'

'But what of you?'

'I'll take yours. We "Saxon scum" are accustomed to riding without a saddle.'

Wilfrid rode to the courtyard in front of the Caen Castle stables, then dismounted and bent double, regaining his breath. King William clattered in shortly after and rode straight up to him, his son William Rufus close on his heels. The king remained in the saddle, grinning down at Wilfrid.

'I am returning this horse, but not to the same man.'

'Sire?'

'I was handed it by a mere knight from somewhere in Norfolk. I now return it to the Earl of Norwich.'

Wilfrid knelt and lowered his head. 'You do me great honour, sire. Although I am reluctant to accept, I shall strive to be deemed worthy of that honour.'

'See that you do,' the king chuckled as he dismounted and walked towards the Great Hall, calling for wine to be served immediately.

The new Earl of Norwich looked up and found himself staring at the sneering face of William Rufus, even redder than usual from the exertion of his recent retreat, as he handed his horse's bridle to the waiting groom.

'Do not grow too comfortable with your ill-gotten prize, Saxon peasant! When I am King of England, all you people shall be made to realise their true place, which is at the bottom of the dung-heap.'

'Then we shall just have to hope that the crown of England goes to someone more deserving than one whose only true talent in life is the emptying of piss-pots,' Wilfrid fired back, before Rufus turned angrily on his heel and stalked off.

Several weeks later, Wilfrid was on his way home, in the retinue of the man he had threatened with his sword at the gates of Gerberoi. Robert had become reconciled with his father Duke William, and had been mollified by the opportunity to lead an army through England in order to deal with the Scots King Malcolm, who had learned of King William of England's forced retreat from what should have been a simple siege, without being advised of why William had stayed his hand. Malcolm had led his Scots warriors as far south as the Tees before it occurred to those in the northernmost portion of King William's kingdom that their monarch was not riding north to defend them.

This was all the encouragement that was needed by those who retained bitter memories of the 'harrowing'. The Bishop of Durham, who was also the recently appointed Earl of Northumbria following the execution of Waltheof, was messily done to death in a popular uprising in which King Malcolm was invited to march further south. It was this threat from the north that Robert had been sent to quell, and he had insisted on taking with him, as a personal bodyguard, the man who had prevented him from killing his father.

The Scots retreated from this massive Norman army faster than their challengers could march. Robert and his men never saw so much as a flash of distant armour as they pushed all the way to the southern outskirts of Edinburgh, where Scots envoys were sent out to seek peace terms. It was to be doubted whether the treacherous Malcolm would honour his vow to remain within his own lands any more than he had the previous ones, but Robert returned south and began work on new fortifications to guard the crossing of the River Tyne, which he named 'New Castle'.

As soon as the wooden structure was roofed, and a great hall of sorts was equipped for dining, Robert Curthose decided to throw a massive banquet for all those who had marched with him to a great victory without the shedding of any blood on either side. Everyone was convincingly drunk on the local ale when Robert turned to Wilfrid, seated to his left, and slurringly asked a question.

'Would you really have killed me, had I continued to threaten my father?'

'Yes. He may be your father, but he is also my king.'

'Do you feel the same loyalty to me? If we had engaged the enemy during this campaign, and had I been in mortal danger, as my father was, would you have done the same thing to protect my life?'

'Of course, since you are my liege lord. Or at least, you are his son, and one day you may be our king.'

'What if your next king proves to be my revolting younger brother William?'

'If he is crowned King, he will of course have my life at his command.'

'Such loyalty! Are all you Saxons the same?'

'I cannot speak for any Saxon other than myself.'

It fell silent for a moment, then Robert gave a mighty belch before continuing. 'I'm sorry I called you "scum" that day at Gerberoi. It's hard to resist the urgings of my younger brother. It's easier to go along with what he demands rather than feel his wrath.'

'It must be even harder for your youngest brother Henry.'

'Indeed, he's terrified of William. But be warned — I have no interest other than in Normandy, and when my father dies, he is likely to leave England to Rufus.'

'Not Henry?'

'Henry is still only in his twelfth year, and more given to book learning than fighting. In Normandy they call him "Beauclerc", in the same way that they call William "Rufus", and me "Curthose". But now I have this urgent pressure in my gut which requires me to leave you in order to throw up somewhere quiet outside.'

Wilfrid left the southbound royal army at Peterborough, and returned home to a somewhat frosty welcome. Instead of rushing out to meet him as she normally did, Joan remained resolutely inside the kitchen, supervising the preparation of supper.

Wilfrid breezed in with arms wide open and called out, 'Behold the Earl of Norwich!'

Joan turned with a blank expression. 'Do I know you?'

Wilfrid laughed nervously. 'I'm sorry it's been so long, but…'

'Save your excuses for the children. They've been mourning your death, since they couldn't think of any reason why you'd be missing for so long.'

'I went to Normandy as planned, then I had to go up north with an army, and…'

'Will it always be like this?'

'Perhaps you'd prefer it if I *were* dead,' Wilfrid huffed back at her. 'That would at least put an end to the wondering.'

Joan seemed to relent as she allowed that thought to sink in. She walked across the kitchen towards him, then stopped. 'Of course not, but you've no idea what it's like, week after week, knowing that your man's out there somewhere fighting battles.

Every time a horse comes through the gate that doesn't have you on its back, I fear that it may be some messenger with news that you've been hacked to pieces and buried in some lonely grave. I remember how you came back that time with Selwyn's body draped over his horse, and…'

Her face crumpled, and Wilfrid raced over to comfort her. As she wrapped her arms round him, she gave way to her tears. The cook slipped tactfully out of the kitchen.

'What was that new title you mentioned?' Joan enquired once the tears had dried.

'Earl of Norwich. King William granted it to me after I saved his life — his oldest son was all set to put a sword through him.'

'Lovely family,' Joan replied sarcastically. 'Does that mean that we have to move? Only Thomas and Elston seem to be learning well under their new tutor, and Elva's finally opened her village school, although it looks more like a home for waifs and strays. There are some village children without proper parents, and she's building onto the side of the convent to give them somewhere to live. If we move out of here for more than a day, she'll turn it into a home for the homeless.'

'We don't necessarily have to move,' Wilfrid reassured her. 'I can leave my own men in command at Norwich Castle, and we can continue to live here. I just need to visit it from time to time, and of course answer the king's call when — and if — it comes.'

'Is that likely to be often?'

'Who can tell? The king spends most of his time in Normandy, quarrelling with his oldest son Robert. While over there, he relies mainly on those of his knights who are Norman by birth to govern England. He rarely returns here, since

England is so peaceful, so perhaps we may look forward to a quiet life here on our estate.'

Wilfrid's predictions held good for the next six years. He appointed his own Captain of the Guard at Norwich Castle, and made only occasional visits, during which everything seemed to be well organised. Such news that he received from Normandy came by way of Richard Fitz Gilbert, who continued to govern England during King William's almost permanent absence. Wilfrid learned that father and son were still at odds, with Philip of France siding with Robert in an effort to weaken his father's grip on Normandy.

The convent founded by Mother Magdalena began to swell in size, as local girls with no prospects of marriage took the veil as the only viable option if they wished to be fed and have a roof over their heads. 'Sister Grace' was placed in charge of the novitiates, who had reached seven in number before the first of them took her final vows. She offered to tend the sick while Grace continued to teach the local children to read and write — but in English rather than French, which seemed to dominate everywhere else in the realm.

Matilda attained her sixteenth birthday in 1083, and to her considerable delight she was invited by her aunt to assist in the work of the school. This also pleased her parents, since she had grown into a tall and self-assured beauty who had a score of male admirers. It was deemed more appropriate that she spent her days in what amounted to religious seclusion, indulging her own scholarly instincts.

As for the boys, Wilfrid looked on with worried frowns as he observed the increasing influence of the oldest of the three, Magdalena's boy Geoffrey, on Thomas and Elston. Wilfrid was obliged to keep reminding himself that Geoffrey's father had been a fierce and combative warrior king — the last Saxon King of England — so it was only natural that this personality trait should predominate over his mother's more docile religious serenity.

Geoffrey seemed to spend his every waking hour on horseback, tilting at imaginary foes that took the form of stuffed sacks hanging from tree branches in the Long Meadow. Wilfrid dreaded any outbreak of warfare in England that might require him to answer the call to arms, since young Geoffrey might campaign to become his squire in his burning desire to progress as a man of warfare. When his bellicose nature began to influence Thomas and Elston, Wilfrid sought to divert their energies by giving them farming responsibilities in and around the estate. But he was fighting a losing battle, and he dreaded the day that Richard Fitz Gilbert arrived through the gate with a command that the Earl of Norwich don his chainmail in the service of the king.

When Fitz Gilbert did arrive, it was with very unsettling news. He advised Wilfrid that when further dissent had broken out between King William and Robert, King Philip of France had stirred things up in the disputed Vexin that lay between Normandy and the French territory of the Île de France. During an attack on Nantes, William's horse had reared up, forcing its saddle pommel into the duke's stomach. Barely a week later, he was dead.

As predicted, Robert had been bequeathed Normandy, while nineteen-year-old Henry had received a sum of money. This meant that England was now ruled by the dissolute and unpredictable William Rufus, who had no love for Wilfrid, and who was in the process of crossing the Channel to claim his crown.

V

It was the twenty-sixth day of September 1087. Wilfrid sat staring down the grassy slope at the shrine in which Sister Grace was conducting her daily instruction of novitiates in front of the Holy statue, trying to persuade himself yet again that staying away from the coronation had been the best course open to him. He of course owed an oath of allegiance to William Rufus, who was in the process of being crowned William II of England in Westminster Abbey at the hand of Archbishop of Canterbury Lanfranc, but there would be time enough for that. Hopefully, Rufus would have forgotten how Wilfrid had hauled him off his younger brother Henry by the seat of his hose.

There were other, and better, ways of showing allegiance, Wilfrid reasoned as he watched the younger men of the village drifting down to the riverbank, the customary meeting place for the weekly arms practice and fitness drill. He was required, as the price of his continued lordship of the Manor of Walsingham, to keep a fyrd of fighting men battle-ready for the king's service, and it should not matter who that king was. At the same time, Wilfrid was concerned in case the manor's young men were committed to service in Normandy — this could happen if William and Robert continued the rivalry in which they had been engaged for the last few years of their father's life. William Rufus had inherited England, and Robert had retained Normandy, but how long before each began casting covetous eyes on the other's inheritance, and threw away thousands of English lives in their bitter quarrels?

'The men are ready,' Thomas advised Wilfrid as he ran up the slope. 'May I lead them off in some warming-up runs down the riverbank?'

'No, you may not,' Wilfrid advised him sternly. 'You may go back down and join them, and be ready for when I come down to take command of the training.'

Thomas slouched away, with a resentful, rejected look on his face. He glared across at Geoffrey, who was striding out of the manor house decked out in half armour. He looked exactly like the professional knight that he aspired to become, once he could find an existing knight who would enlist him as a squire. At twenty-two, he was already older than Wilfrid had been when, as 'Will Riveracre', he had formed the Sandlake Fyrd that had stood against Duke William's forces at Senlac. It was clearly only a matter of time before Geoffrey achieved his ambition and was returned to Mother Magdalena as a corpse draped across a saddle.

There was no obvious way to prevent Geoffrey from going to an almost certain death in the heroic tradition, but Wilfrid was damned if he was going to allow his nineteen-year-old son Thomas to go the same way. The rivalry that had always existed between Thomas and Geoffrey had, if anything, grown stronger over the years. Wilfrid might well have to tie Thomas down with ropes to keep him imprisoned at home if Geoffrey ever achieved his ambition, then taunted Thomas into outdoing him. Not for the first time, Wilfrid wished that Thomas had grown up more like Elston, and shown more interest in learning. Even if Elston finished up as a humble priest in some obscure parish or monastery, at least he would still be alive. It was unlikely that Sister Grace would mourn the absence of grandchildren, given the devotion she displayed towards her novitiates and orphans.

Weapons training came to its usual halt when the first of the winter gales became flecked with sleet, which a week later became heavy snow on an unforgiving easterly wind. The harvest was in, and folk kept to their own firesides with their salted provisions, rarely showing their faces over the threshold. The only social interaction was between the manor house and the much-expanded convent buildings that lay in a cluster a few yards away, their largest room being the chapel that had begun life as the accommodation wing of the old manor house. Wilfrid and Joan's daughter, Matilda, although not yet committed to taking holy orders, had opted to move in with the novitiates in the convent, from which it was more convenient to conduct her classes for the children in the orphanage attached to the main convent.

One evening, Matilda joined her parents for supper and could barely contain her excitement as she shook the snow from her cloak. She hung it on the wooden peg by the door and scurried in to warm her hands and feet by the blazing fire.

'Archbishop Lanfranc is paying us a visit in a few weeks!' she announced breathlessly.

'What does *he* want?' her father enquired without any enthusiasm.

'He's the Archbishop of Canterbury!' Matilda reminded him.

'I know who he is,' Wilfrid replied. 'My question was, what does he want?'

'Father!' Matilda chided him. 'Have you forgotten that the Shrine of Our Lady of Walsingham is now considered the most holy shrine in England? He's coming here on a pilgrimage.'

'Will we need to give him accommodation here in the manor house?' Joan enquired with a worried frown.

'We don't have a dedicated *hospitium* in the convent,' Matilda explained, 'but Mother Magdalena has offered to give up her own room for his comfort.'

'It still doesn't sound like a good idea for an archbishop to be sleeping in a convent,' Wilfrid observed. 'What about his retinue?'

'He's just bringing his chaplain, apparently,' Matilda advised them, 'but if Mother Magdalena has to give up her room, we'll need to house her in here.'

'I'll get Martha to open up the upstairs rooms,' Joan offered. 'We need to get the crows out of their winter roosts anyway. It's as well that we had them built on, all the same.'

Once the snow had ceased, and the country tracks were made passable again by those who bravely ventured along them first, the family made the last-minute preparations, and were not taken unawares when two heavily draped horse-borne figures plodded through the entrance towards the manor house. Wilfrid stepped out from the front doorway as the first of the riders pulled on his reins, jumped down from his horse, threw back the cloak that had been covering his head to reveal the grey remnants of an elderly tonsure, and assisted the other man off his horse. The second, larger man also threw back his riding hood, and smiled warmly at his host. He had clear blue eyes and a wind-reddened face.

Before Wilfrid could hold out a hand in welcome, he was overtaken by two black-robed women, flapping like startled crows to be the first to kneel and kiss the ring on the outstretched hand as some sort of blessing was mumbled over their heads. Mother Magdalena led the way down to the shrine, outside which the nine members of the convent were introduced individually, and were offered the opportunity to kiss the ring.

'It's a wonder that ring isn't worn down to his knuckle,' Wilfrid observed sardonically, before Joan reminded him that their guest was one of the most powerful men in England, and an emissary of the Pope.

'You always were more religiously inclined than me,' Wilfrid responded with a smile. 'Which reminds me — where's Elston?'

'In the house, preparing to be introduced by Elva, once she sends her novitiates back into their dormitory.'

An hour later, the introductions were complete. The mulled wine was flowing freely as the housemaid Wendel kept circulating with the jug through the group gathered around the fire. Archbishop Lanfranc was in an expansive mood.

'Your shrine really is an inspiration to the entire Christian world,' he announced, 'and Mother Magdalena is to be congratulated on her fine achievement in establishing her convent. One can only assume that the Blessed Virgin herself is content with the growing attention being given to the Christian faith by those attracted here. When next I am in Rome, I shall commend to his Holiness that the new house she founded be recognised as a religious order.'

'Is it not already?' Joan queried.

Lanfranc shook his head. 'Until the Pope gives his blessing, it cannot be acknowledged as a convent belonging to an established order, entitled to the privileges that attend such an institution.'

'Such as?' Wilfrid enquired.

'That may well become a matter of some argument in future,' Lanfranc began. 'Under the previous king, who was a devout Christian, the holy houses were exempt from taxation, and were allowed to retain their own income from the estates that they hold. That clearly is not an issue here, since I am advised that the convent that Mother Magdalena founded has never been required to pay feudal dues to the manor in which it is located.'

'It is we who are indebted to the former Lady Richeldis,' Wilfrid explained, 'since it was she who gave us sanctuary some years ago, before the manor was granted to me. Once I became the lord of the manor, the least I could do was allow the convent to be formed, free of any charge from the manor.'

Lanfranc smiled. 'You are to be commended for your generosity once your fortunes were reversed, but unfortunately it is not the same in other parts of the nation, where there are endless squabbles between the nobles and the clergy over matters such as the collection of feudal dues and the jurisdiction of the manor courts. In some manors, the lord insists on trying clergy in his own court for their offences, rather than allowing the Church courts to deal with them.'

'I'm surprised to learn that clergymen commit offences,' Wilfrid observed.

'I'm not,' Joan replied with a faint shudder.

'Be that as it may,' Lanfranc continued, as if there had been no interruption, 'our new king has made it known that he does not share his father's devotion to Christ, and that he regards himself as being above those who have been ordained. He insists that religious establishments must pay their taxes just like his feudal nobles, and that even ordained priests — and even higher members of the English Church such as myself — are subject to his laws. Even his own half-uncle Odo, who was once the Bishop of Bordeaux, and who fought alongside the first William during the invasion battle.'

'I remember him,' Wilfrid replied with a grimace. 'A terrifying sight in his bishop's robes over his chainmail, swinging a massive axe and lopping off heads as if they were sheafs of corn.'

'Yes, his final encounter with God will be an interesting event,' Lanfranc smiled mischievously. 'But he has a more immediate battle ahead of him, as Earl of Kent under his half-nephew William Rufus.'

'In what way?' Wilfrid enquired.

Lanfranc lowered his voice conspiratorially. 'The enmity between King William and his brother Count Robert of Normandy has presented some of the more prominent English nobles with a dilemma. They obviously owe allegiance for their English lands to William, but equally obviously they must do obeisance to Robert for lands they hold in Normandy. Should either brother declare war on the other, where do their loyalties lie? It has been suggested that they choose now which of the brothers to give their loyalty to, and effectively foreswear their other lands, but what nobleman would voluntarily forfeit half his estates? There is, in consequence, a growing preference for one brother to be supported in overthrowing the other, who will — like their father — therefore become the sovereign lord of both nations. As things stand, the preference is likely to be for Robert.'

'I must own that I found him to be the more pleasant of the two brothers, during my very short time in the company of them both,' Wilfrid admitted. 'I even rode at Robert's side when he drove back Malcolm of Scotland from our northern borders. But I also informed him that should William become our king, I would be duty-bound to support him, and he seemed to accept that — even to admire it.'

'Your clear-minded loyalty is indeed to be commended,' Lanfranc advised him, 'but it may well be tested in the months to come.'

'How?'

'You owe immediate homage to Roger Bigod, do you not?'

Wilfrid shrugged his shoulders in indecision. 'The point has not been raised in recent years, since there has been no need for my feudal lord to call for knight service. My only knightly service has been under the direct command of a king or one of his sons. My original lord was Earl Waltheof, who was executed for his rebellion, and I was created Earl of Norwich at around the same time. In that capacity I obviously answer directly to King William, if called upon, but I don't know if there's anyone in between.'

Lanfranc thought briefly, then gave his opinion. 'Roger Bigod is a Godless man, much given to wild debauching, gambling and other pursuits that make him a personal favourite of William's. He's currently Sheriff of Norfolk, among his other titles, and as Sheriff he carries the royal writ around the King's Courts. Should he issue you with any command, you would be obliged to obey it, as I understand the common law.'

'If it comes originally from King William, why would I not obey it?'

Lanfranc leaned closer and dropped his voice. 'Bigod is said to be in league with Odo of Kent to stage a rebellion against William's rule in England, and to invite Robert to invade.'

Wilfrid smiled reassuringly. 'This is not the first time that I have been confronted by such a dilemma. During the barons' revolt against the former King William, my feudal overlord was Earl Waltheof, but I was advised by the Justiciar Fitz Gilbert to refuse to obey any call to arms by him, and to await further orders from the king via his justiciar. May I not simply ignore any command to arms by Bigod, and instead hold out for the king?'

'A very honourable course, if it may be safely pursued,' Lanfranc replied with a frown. 'Bigod is nearer to you in distance than the king, who is either in London or Winchester for the most part. If Bigod chooses to exact reprisals for your refusal to join his rebellion, you may wait a long time for King William to come to your relief.'

'That is a risk I must run,' Wilfrid replied firmly. 'At least by remaining loyal to the king I will not lose my lands or be executed as a traitor.'

'Assuming that you live,' Lanfranc reminded him. 'Would you be prepared to die for William?'

'Not for William the man,' Wilfrid replied, 'for I find him detestable as a person, whereas Robert is more reasonable. I would myself much prefer that Robert be our king, but so long as William wears the crown, then as I see it I must defend him. Otherwise, the nation will be thrown into even more chaos than it has known these past twenty or so years.'

'Would that everyone was as honourable and clear-thinking,' Lanfranc smiled. 'But now I see that the board has been laid, and that I am expected to pronounce the blessing over what appears to be a delightful supper. Please sit by me, and tell me more about the influence that your neighbouring shrine has over your manor and its people.'

VI

The summer was almost upon them when Wilfrid next had occasion to recall Lanfranc's warning. Late one afternoon, a familiar figure clattered noisily through the manor estate gate, jumped from his horse without making any effort to tie it up or lead it to the stables, and strode rapidly over to where Wilfrid was sharpening his old sword, for want of anything else to do. The returning warrior was now the Captain of the Guard at Norwich Castle, part of Wilfrid's earldom.

Before being elevated to Captain of the Norwich Guard, the man in question had been Enric of Huntingdon, one of those selected by Waltheof to form the first armed body under Wilfrid's command at Walsingham, when the manor had still belonged to Richeldis de Faverches. Enric had then been chosen by Wilfrid to lead the small armed contingent he had trained as best he could, primarily because he was feared by all the other men: Enric had murdered, with his bare hands, a man who had ravished his ten-year-old daughter. He had been pardoned by the earl in return for his agreement to defend Walsingham, and had since moved his family, first to Wilfrid's village, then behind the palisade of Norwich Castle, from which he had now returned with urgent news.

'A man calling himself Sheriff Bigod of Norfolk has commanded that we hand over the castle,' Enric announced somewhat breathlessly.

'But you have not done so?' Wilfrid enquired.

Enric shook his head. 'You are my commander, my lord, and I told the man that I would need to ride here to obtain your instructions.'

53

'Excellent,' Wilfrid replied as he thought quickly. 'Rest here for the night with friends — or, if not, we can accommodate you in the manor house. Tomorrow I'll ride back with you to Norwich. You can then return here with your family in order to guard the manor and continue to train the men who remain here. I'll take over command of the castle for a brief while, then we can once again exchange places. I'll leave my family here while I'm away, and it will be your responsibility to protect them as well as the rest of the village.'

They rode out shortly after daybreak the following morning, with Joan's protests still ringing in their ears. By the middle of the following day, Wilfrid had doubled the guard on duty at any time around the walls of Norwich Castle. Then he sat and waited. Three days later, Sheriff Bigod appeared at the gate demanding audience with Wilfrid, and the two of them withdrew to a table in the main hall with a jug of wine.

'You have King William's authority for me to yield my castle?' Wilfrid enquired. 'And if so, on what grounds have I been deemed no longer worthy to hold it?'

Bigod smiled unpleasantly, resembling a cat in pain. 'I do not need William's authority, for two reasons. The first is that I am sheriff of this county, and I carry the royal writ of authority wherever I ride. The second is that William Rufus will not be King of England for much longer.'

'He is ill?' Wilfrid enquired disingenuously.

The smile disappeared from Bigod's face. 'I was warned that you were tricky, so I will be blunt. There will shortly be a rebellion against William's rule, in favour of Count Robert his brother, and either you hand this castle over to me immediately, or you swear a vow to hold it in the cause of that rebellion.'

'And if I do neither?'

'Then I take the castle from you using armed force.'

'I will honour your frankness by being equally frank in my response,' Wilfrid glared back at him. 'You have safe passage from my castle on this occasion, but don't return. I cannot be swayed from my loyalty to the lawfully crowned king from whom I hold this castle.'

Bigod rose quickly and angrily from the table. 'When he is no longer king, you will be hanged as a traitor to King Robert.'

'I cannot commit treason against a man while he is not my king,' Wilfrid pointed out. 'Until he is, I owe allegiance to the man who is king at this time.'

'Stupid peasant upstart!' Bigod roared down at him as he turned to leave.

The two armed men at the door unsheathed their swords and left their posts, moving towards him, but Wilfrid waved his hand in a delaying gesture.

'Let him depart without harm. And so I bid you good day, my lord Sheriff.'

Bigod strode between the two guards and opened the door. With a final yell, he slammed it shut, and all fell quiet.

Wilfrid waited a month, during which time there was no further sign of Bigod, then he rode back to Walsingham and changed places once again with Enric. Joan waited two days before she finally admitted that she was relieved to see Wilfrid safely home, and secured from him a promise that in future, wherever he went, she would be allowed to travel with him.

'After all,' she argued, 'the children are all grown, and no longer need parents. And if you're going to die, I'd rather be there to hold you in my arms for your last few minutes of life. I think that's what still hurts Elva the most — that she wasn't able to kiss Selwyn goodbye.'

Having conceded the point, Wilfrid waited anxiously for news of the rebellion. It came irregularly and by different routes, mainly via village gossip. So far as could be deduced from the snippets of information that they received, the rebellion had broken out in various parts of the nation, but had focused mainly on Kent, the stronghold of Odo. He was best placed to give a safe landing to Robert's intended invasion force.

Then it was learned that Pevensey Castle was under siege, and Wilfrid was sorely tempted to ride there himself, in case the village of his birth, Sandlake, which lay within sight of Pevensey, might be in danger. But Joan managed to talk him out of that, and the next news was that Pevensey had fallen to William's besieging force, that Odo was William's prisoner, and that Robert's hoped-for invasion fleet had failed to cross the Channel due to bad weather. The remaining rebels fell back on Rochester, then gave up their rebellion as a lost cause when several of its leaders were offered generous terms if they would acknowledge William as their liege lord.

Three months later, early in 1089, Wilfrid was summoned to the Court at Westminster by a messenger, who made it clear that the invitation was not optional. Wilfrid and Joan argued long into the night over whether or not she might accompany him, since this would be the first test of his vow to take her with him wherever he went in future.

'But that was only in case I might be facing danger, so you could be there at my death,' he said triumphantly as Joan ran out of counter-arguments. 'What danger can there be on this occasion? The king no doubt intends to reward me in some way for holding firm and not handing over Norwich to Bigod, who has probably been put to death by now.'

'How long will you be away?' Joan pouted as she conceded the point.

'No more than two weeks, I would imagine. I'll obviously visit Enric and the men at arms at Norwich, and stay there overnight. I'll probably change horses there, then it will require only one more overnight stay until I reach Westminster. I'll remember it fondly on your behalf.'

'The only fond memories I have of Westminster involve you,' Joan replied as a tear began to form in the corner of her eye, 'so take care.'

With considerable reluctance and foreboding, Joan kissed Wilfrid goodbye as he climbed onto his horse and trotted him out of the estate. He spent two nights in Norwich, before pointing his refreshed horse south on the track to London.

Much had changed at the Palace of Westminster. The first, and most noticeable, difference was that on Will Riveracre's first visit to the old West Minster, it had been full of serving girls scurrying back and forth with platters of food and flagons of wine. Joan had been one of these, and they had mixed freely with the housecarls, resulting in many marriages or other less formal relationships. Now these serving girls appeared to have been replaced by serving boys: brightly dressed young men in longer tunics that appeared to be all the fashion.

But a far greater shock awaited Wilfrid on the following day, when he was announced by a piping-voiced usher. Wilfrid advanced towards the throne, then dropped to one knee in the required manner before looking back up at the man on the throne, who was barely recognisable as the young man who had sneered at him from atop a horse at Gerberoi.

Not only did he look ten years older, but King William's face was no longer the pudgy product of youth. His previously unkempt ginger hair appeared to have been lightened in some way, so that now it was a golden colour. However, this might have been the effect of a reflected glow from the yellow ribbon tied through his carefully combed locks, or the occasional jewel that glistened under the candles from not only his hair, but around his neck and on various parts of his tunic. The tunic was longer than the previous fashion, and beneath it William wore gold-coloured hose that ended at the knee, revealing his bare calves as they tapered down towards an extravagant pair of heeled slippers.

Rufus was almost outshone by the group seated around him, one of whom William realised with a start was Roger Bigod. Like Rufus, they all wore ridiculously and impracticably long tunics down to their knees, with calves exposed to view beneath shorn-off hose of various hues, all of them garish. Several of them — including Bigod — were sporting jewels in their hair, and as Wilfrid knelt there he was overtaken by the uncomfortable feeling that he was being inspected like a prize mare.

'You took your time about it,' Rufus complained as he rose from his throne. 'But it was worth the wait. You've retained your youthful look, even though you must be well into your late thirties.'

'Forty this year, sire.'

'Really? I hope I look as — well, as *active* as you do — when I reach that age. It must be all that country air up in Norfolk. It's certainly done a great deal for my good friend Roger here, hasn't it?'

He waved a hand in the general direction of Roger Bigod, who glared down at Wilfrid from a padded seat close to the king's.

Rufus smiled at them both. 'I hope that you two will remain good friends in the future, since Roger here has promised me that he'll never again rebel. I realise that you were showing your loyalty to me when you refused to hand over that castle in Norwich, but now you must give it back to him.'

'*Back* to him, sire?' Wilfrid echoed in stunned disbelief.

Rufus stretched out a languid arm in order to touch Bigod on the shoulder. 'I've made him Earl of Norfolk, since he's been good, and he tells me that he wants to live in Norwich Castle. I hope you're not going to be difficult about giving up your title to it? Since you did what you thought was best at the time, you can of course keep your manor estates. Just not Norwich Castle, *understood*?'

There was such a tone of menace in the delivery of that last word that Wilfrid was left in no doubt that despite his loyalty, he had just been stripped of both the castle and the earldom that the new king's father had granted him. He nodded in a silent gesture of submission, afraid to speak in case he said things that would separate him from his head.

Rufus smiled. 'Good. Run away and play, now.'

Wilfrid rode away from Westminster confused, embarrassed, outraged and humiliated. He covered the distance back to Norwich in half the time it had taken to ride south. As his exhausted horse was led, limping badly, to the stables, he called for Enric, and ordered him to muster all the Walsingham men who wished to return home, and march them away as soon as could be arranged.

'What about the safety of the castle, my lord?' Enric enquired hesitantly.

'Never mind the castle!' Wilfrid spat back. 'It's no longer mine. The Devil may take it — along with the treacherous dog who now has command of it, and the pathetic king who seems incapable of recognising true loyalty!'

VII

The Shrine of Our Lady of Walsingham was now receiving so many visiting pilgrims that Mother Magdalena had been obliged to use some of the offertory money to build a *hospitium* in which those visiting from a long distance might be accommodated. Increasingly, such visitors were clerics of various denominations and degrees, and Wilfrid was therefore hardly surprised to see the Holy Mother walking towards him from the convent buildings to the manor house with a monk alongside her. But he was a little intrigued when she stopped and introduced her visitor.

'Wilfrid, this is Brother Ignatius from the Abbey of Ely. He is not just here to visit the shrine — he requires your assistance and advice.'

'I'm hardly qualified to be giving spiritual guidance.' Wilfrid bowed slightly in acknowledgment of the elderly cowled figure that stood before him. 'That's your task, surely?'

'It's obviously not a spiritual matter,' Magdalena smiled back graciously. 'It concerns the threat to the continued existence of the abbey itself.'

'You are seeking a monetary donation?' Wilfrid enquired lightly.

Brother Ignatius gave him a tired smile. 'No, my lord. Rather some advice regarding a temporal matter. Or rather, a matter that should be spiritual, but which the king seems determined to deal with as if he is above God.'

Wilfrid indicated for the monk to take a seat beside him on the bench outside the manor house, and invited him to explain.

Ignatius cleared his throat. 'The great Abbey of Ely was the inspired work of our former Abbot Simeon, who began work on a magnificent cathedral before his recent death. God granted him a long life, given his holy works, and he was one hundred years old when God finally called him home. Then, when the governance of the abbey fell vacant on his death, it was seized, on the orders of King William, by his evilly inspired Keeper of the Royal Seal, Ranulf Flambard. He has claimed all our revenues for the king, and we are reduced to penury. We have no-one to whom to make our protest, since there has been no Archbishop of Canterbury since the death of Lanfranc. The king refuses to recognise the jurisdiction of our Church courts, claiming that all matters of law are for the King's Justices to determine. He imprisoned the Bishop of Durham because he would not yield his castle, and he was denied the right to appeal to Rome because the king insisted that even those matters of law involving senior clerics belong in the royal courts.'

'I suggested that the monks of Ely appeal to Rome,' Mother Magdalena added, 'but it seems that the king does not recognise the authority of the Pope in matters which he regards as rightly belonging under his grace and favour. Which, these days, apparently means everything.'

'But what assistance do you think I can render?' Wilfrid protested. 'The lands of Ely do not lie within my manor — who is your temporal lord?'

'The abbey lies within the manor of Stretham,' Ignatius explained, 'but the previous lord died some years ago, and the king has refused to recognise his son as his successor. By these means, the evil Flambard controls the revenues not only of our holy house, but also the manor that lies within its curtilage. I have been asked to seek your assistance, since it is rumoured that you defeated the wicked Hereward when he set up camp on the island that exists within that manor.'

'That much is true,' Wilfrid conceded, 'although I did not do so alone, and I had the blessing of the former king. As I understand it, you are seeking a way of defying his son now that he has inherited the throne. I have to advise you that my dealings with him thus far have been such that not only would he ignore any representations I made on your behalf, but he would probably have me locked inside the new Tower downstream from Westminster.'

'So you can do nothing to help us?'

'With considerable regret, no, I cannot. I can only add, for all the consolation it might be, that I have formed the lowest opinion of our latest king. I once thought his father to be evil, but at least he recognised the authority of God and the Pope.'

'Where will all this end?' Mother Magdalena mused.

'In Hell, for King Rufus,' Wilfrid replied. 'As for the rest of us, who knows?'

Wilfrid was still feeling guilty over his inability to intervene with the king in the matter of Ely when he was approached by Mother Magdalena late one afternoon. He was preparing to oversee the arms training that he had deputed to Magdalena's son Geoffrey, who was already standing proudly at the riverbank, counting the men in. Magdalena took the seat next to his on the long bench where he had recently spoken with Brother Ignatius, and she reached out to place her cool hand on his wrist.

'I was clearly inspired by God when I agreed to give you and your two families sanctuary here. We now have a well-defended manor in which the shrine has thrived, with my own son now being allowed to rise to some sort of leadership in its defence. His father would have been proud.'

'*We* were the ones who were blessed by God, in being offered this sanctuary,' Wilfrid replied reassuringly. 'Had we remained in the wilderness that was England in those days, we would have been swept up in the bloodshed. The Conqueror had difficulty in distinguishing one Saxon from another. As for Geoffrey's father, I have never once lost sight of the fact that he was the last Saxon King of England, who I once served, and I do my utmost to continue to serve the cause he stood for. Not the Saxon cause, that is — simply the right of all men to live in peace under a just and strong ruler, regardless of the lineage of the king who reigns at any given time.'

'Brave words,' Magdalena muttered, 'but will anything prevent my only son from pursuing his dream to be a knight? And if he does, how long will he live?'

'Does he know who his father was?'

'I have not told him. As far as I know, there are very few left who remember "Edith Swan Neck", as I was before I became the Lady Richeldis. This is now my third identity, as the head of a convent. But you must surely have seen for yourself how the blood of Geoffrey's father runs through his veins. He is a born warrior, and I keep him here like a tame bull.'

'I grow old, and weaker by the month,' Wilfrid advised her sadly. 'I would be happy to hand over the full control of our local fyrd to Geoffrey.'

Magdalena smiled. 'We do not hear that word — "fyrd" — too often these days. It might be better to call it something else, since our present king appears to dislike anything Saxon as much as his father did, although he granted you this manor and your title.'

'It was his way of thanking me for ridding him of Hereward, although even now I would gladly hand it back, were it possible to restore Selwyn's life.'

'Do you miss him so much?'

'Of course — he was like a brother to me. But I would imagine that my sister Elva keeps him even closer in her heart and her memory. Does she ever speak of him?'

'Never as such, since she has taken so well to the religious life.'

'It is always a sad reminder to me, when I look down the slope towards Selwyn's grave, that for all the honour and pride of being a knight, or even a squire, you walk daily with death as a companion.' Wilfrid watched Geoffrey lunging at an imagined adversary. He was teaching the manoeuvre to land labourers, millers and cowherds.

'I am aware of that,' Magdalena replied with a slight shudder, 'and I pray daily to God for guidance in the matter of Geoffrey's future. But the words I hear in my head are always the same. They tell me I must allow my son his freedom, and give my blessing for him to go out in the world to seek his future as a warrior. For all that I sometimes lie awake at night crying because I have, in my dreams, been back on that awful battlefield, looking down at the mutilated remains of the only man I ever loved, I feel that I must let Geoffrey go. I believe that the time is now right.'

'Why now in particular?'

'As you know, we are graced by the arrival here of many clergymen from around the world,' Magdalena explained. 'Of late, those who have travelled here for many weeks from parts across the Channel have talked about the imminent collapse of the Byzantine Empire and its Church, which is of course linked to our own Church of Rome. If Constantinople falls to the

Turks, the road of pilgrims to the holy places such as Jerusalem will be forever blocked. It is rumoured that Pope Urban is seeking to persuade Christian kings to send warriors to defend our Christian heritage, and it might be fitting if Geoffrey were to be one of them.'

Wilfrid sat deep in thought, alarmed by what he was hearing. 'It is to be doubted that our king will answer such a call. He defies not only the Pope, but God himself, by all accounts. Why would he agree to send armed men to the defence of Constantinople, when he would rather employ them against his own brother Robert, with whom he is still in dispute regarding the suzerainty of Normandy?'

'You have summarised the position well, insofar as an aging old nun can assess it,' Magdalena replied. 'But last week, one of our visitors was from a Benedictine house near Caen. He said that Duke Robert of Normandy is likely to answer any call to arms that comes from the Pope.'

'And you think that Geoffrey might journey to join him?' Wilfrid probed. 'He doesn't even speak French, so far as I am aware. He would be completely unknown were he to appear at Robert's Court, a solitary wanderer with no title, no knighthood, and no battle experience.'

It fell silent, but Wilfrid knew Magdalena well enough to appreciate that this was not the end of the conversation.

'How strong is your faith, Wilfrid? I recall the early days, when you first beheld the shrine. There was a light in your eyes, and the occasional tear, as if you were overcome by the beauty of the statue, and what it represented.'

'What is it you seek from me?'

'Your faith, your commitment to God, and a written introduction for Geoffrey. In addition, your only son, just as the Blessed Virgin gave hers.'

Wilfrid stared straight ahead as he fought with his emotions. 'I think I always knew that this day would come,' he muttered after a long silence. 'To what do you wish me to commit Thomas?'

'The same cause as Geoffrey. The rescue of Christendom from the hands of heathen hordes. He is almost as strong in the sword arm. And he speaks French, thanks to your foresight and teaching. He and Geoffrey are like brothers — they even *fight* like brothers.'

'Have you spoken with Joan?'

'That task I leave to you, if you are agreeable to what I urge upon you.'

'Do you honestly believe, in your heart, that it is God's will?'

'I would not be committing Geoffrey if I did not. He is all I have left in this material world.'

It fell painfully silent again, during which Magdalena fiddled with the folds of her vestments.

Eventually, Wilfrid gave a faint nod. 'Very well, I will speak with Joan.'

'Turn and face me,' Magdalena requested.

Wilfrid did so, and was pleasantly surprised to feel a cool liquid being sprinkled over his head as Magdalena intoned some impassioned words over him. Tears rolled down her face.

'That was a blessing with holy water, dearest Wilfrid. Let us pray to God that *He* also blesses what we are about.'

Joan screamed when Wilfrid put the proposal to her, so loudly that Matilda ran in from the convent next door in the belief that her mother had suffered some accident. When she saw only her father and mother confronting each other in the main hall, she hesitated, fearful in case her father had behaved like so many other men and had struck his wife. Joan looked to her for support.

'Your father plans to send Thomas to his death!'

Matilda looked aghast at Wilfrid, and he hastened to explain.

'Mother Magdalena wishes Geoffrey to journey to Normandy, and there enlist with Duke Robert's army to save the Christian Church in Constantinople from heathens who are threatening to overthrow it.'

'What does that have to do with my brother?' Matilda demanded.

'She wishes Thomas to travel with Geoffrey, as his interpreter and companion.'

'And will Thomas also be taking up arms?' Matilda demanded.

'If Geoffrey does, do you think that Thomas will not?' Wilfrid replied sadly. 'They are forever challenging each other to dangerous pursuits, like that time up the great oak tree.'

'Tell him no, Tilly,' Joan demanded, her face streaked with tears.

'I cannot tell either my father or my brother how they must lead their lives,' Matilda explained patiently. 'And what does Thomas say?'

'He says "yes"!' came a jubilant voice from the servant's entrance. Thomas walked into the kitchen.

'Why aren't you at weapons training?' Wilfrid demanded.

Thomas smirked. 'Geoffrey told me what his mother had asked of you. I came back as quickly as I could, to seek to persuade you, and to promise Mother that I'll come back alive.'

'Is there anyone in this family who's prepared to prevent my only son being killed just like his uncle?' Joan wailed.

Thomas crossed the hall to enclose her in his arms. 'Father took up arms before he was twenty, and survived the full might of an invading army. Then he rid the nation of a brigand that not even the king could defeat, and again he survived.'

'But Uncle Selwyn *didn't*, remember,' Joan interrupted.

'He unwisely took to the field while he was still nursing a wound,' Thomas countered, and Wilfrid regretted, not for the first time, having described every minute of the encounter with Hereward when badgered into it by his eager son. 'I am wiser than that,' Thomas added, 'and how far do you think Geoffrey will get in Normandy without any knowledge of French?'

'I am more concerned with how far *you* will get, when those men come at you with their implements of death,' Joan wailed.

Having been granted leave to depart, Geoffrey and Thomas lost no time in making their preparations. A week later — after the predictable sobbing from Joan, the heartfelt blessings of Geoffrey's mother in both her capacities, the warm hug of farewell from Matilda and the shy waves from the women of the convent — the two men trotted out of the manor gate to the muted clapping and best wishes of the entire manor community. More than one estate woman wiped a furtive tear from her eye as the object of their unspoken affection disappeared down the track to Norwich on a large horse that might, or might not, prove suitable for armed combat. As the men disappeared from sight, Wilfrid walked slowly down the grass slope, entered the shrine, fell to his knees, and prayed harder than ever before in his life.

VIII

It had been a close call this time, but King William was now back on his feet. He was already bitterly regretting his uncharacteristic moment of weakness when, believing himself to be on the point of death, he had summoned Christendom's most revered cleric, Anselm of Bec, to hear his final confession and administer the last rites. Not only had the saintly old man been unable to suppress his gasps of horror and disgust while his pious ears were filled with accounts of William's lust, his many acts of blasphemy, and his voracious acquisition of estates and revenues rightly due to religious houses, but he had agreed to accept the see of Canterbury only on his own terms.

There had been ungracious scenes during the reluctant investiture ceremony at Canterbury, when the elderly and much admired theologian had the crozier forced into his unwilling grasp by a group of over-enthusiastic monks from the nearby monastic chapter. He had then been carried bodily into the nave of his own church to the strains of a *Te Deum* sung by the rest of their house, where he was anointed, whether he liked it or not, by the Bishop of Durham in the fastest investiture that the ancient cathedral had ever hosted.

Still unsure in his own mind whether or not he was now the most powerful and influential Churchman in England, Anselm had then dictated to William the conditions upon which he would carry out the duties of the office, in order to avoid the retribution of the Pope for the continued delay in appointing a successor to Lanfranc, who had died four years previously. William didn't especially fear excommunication from the mercy of a God of whose very existence he was not entirely convinced. However, he did fear the forces of the Holy Roman Emperor Henry of Germany, who was currently engaged on the side of the so-called 'anti-Pope' Clement III in a dispute with the official Pope, Urban II. For this reason, King William was reluctant when his newly invested Archbishop of Canterbury demanded, as a term of accepting office, that William denounce Clement as a usurper and a heretic. It had suited William that there were two claimants to the Papal office, since then he could ignore both of them.

William finally conceded the point with bad grace, but dug in when Anselm demanded that William hand back all the Church lands and revenues seized in recent years, in the king's name, by the ambitious royal favourite (and alleged bed partner) Ranulf Flambard. He compromised in the matter of Canterbury itself, which he gave back to Anselm as a personal gift, fully aware that the 'pious old fool' would immediately pass it on to the cathedral office bearers to hold in perpetuity for the benefit of the see.

But they argued most vociferously over King William's insistence that all his subjects, including clergymen of all degrees and distinction, were subject to his courts, and could not claim the benefit of their own system of justice. He was not impressed by Anselm's insistence that anyone ordained in the Church who committed, for example, the crime of murder, would be punished by excommunication from the Grace of God, and would suffer the torments of Hell upon their death. Rather, William insisted, such a man should be put to death instantly and publicly, for the general good, and God could have what was left. It was not, of course, all about mortal sin anyway — it was more a matter of control, and in particular rulings regarding taxes and other revenues, concerning which any royal sheriff or justice could be relied upon to know where his best career interests lay.

Duke Robert read the scroll carefully, then looked back up at the dust-streaked, eager-faced young men who knelt before him.

'Which of you is Thomas Walsingham?' he enquired.

Thomas rose to his feet. 'I am, my lord.'

Robert smiled. 'I should perhaps have guessed. You are the taller of the two, your face resembles that of your father as I remember it, and your French is good. Did your father tell you that he once hauled the current King of England off our younger brother by the seat of his hose?'

'Indeed he did, my Lord,' Thomas replied.

Robert looked across at Geoffrey and asked him a complex question in French. When Geoffrey looked blank, Robert looked back at Thomas with a smile. 'Your companion calls himself Geoffrey de Faverches, a French name, yet he has no French?'

'Regrettably not, my Lord,' said Thomas. 'That is why I have accompanied him to your lands.'

'You are not a warrior yourself?'

'That remains to be seen, my Lord. For myself, I would claim to be as good as Geoffrey here, but I am advised that the letter of introduction offers only his services in your army to relieve Constantinople. For some reason, my own father dismisses my eagerness to fight.'

'Perhaps he seeks to save your life,' Robert replied. 'Does my brother King William know of your journey into my service?'

'I do not believe so, my Lord, nor did I think that we required his approval.'

Robert laughed lightly, and gestured for Geoffrey to rise from the kneeling position that he had maintained throughout the conversation. He then indicated for both young men to take one of the available seats by his side, and called for wine to be served.

'How did you come to learn of my intention to ride to the aid of the Christians in Byzantium?' he enquired of Thomas.

'I learned from the Mother of the Holy Shrine of Walsingham, who is Geoffrey's mother, and she in turn heard it from pilgrims journeying from Normandy.'

'Did she also advise you that currently I lack the funds with which to equip an army?'

'No, she did not.'

'Unfortunately, that is the case. But be of good cheer, because I believe that my brother-in-law Stephen of Blois has the money, but not the fighting men. I will send you to him with my recommendation that you be drafted into his service, perhaps as squires in his immediate retinue. Once knighted, you may of course assemble your own forces. In the meantime, you must serve under one who has proved himself in battle.'

'He is your brother-in-law, you say?' Thomas repeated.

'Indeed. He is married to my sister Adela, and he is most eager to seek fame in the Holy Land. He will be one of the leading commanders when our combined armies move east in due course. But first I must raise the necessary money to equip my part of what will hopefully prove to be the largest single body of fighting men under the banner of the Pope that Christendom has ever seen.'

'The Pope has given it his blessing?'

'He intends to, at a council he will be calling somewhere here in France. We shall all be warriors for Christ. Rest here for as long as you wish, and then present yourselves at Blois.'

IX

'I have already paid my annual dues to Bigod,' Wilfrid complained to the royal official who had arrived unannounced, and who had refused to go away until he had a reason for Wilfrid's attitude, 'so why should I pay an extra tithe?'

'Because the king demands it,' the official replied, as if the answer were obvious.

'And if the king demands that I cut off my right hand, am I to do that also?' Wilfrid demanded. 'Why does he need it, anyway? Has he run out of holy houses to steal from?'

'He intends to take a lease of Normandy,' the official told him.

Wilfrid burst out laughing. 'And what does Duke Robert intend to do when he does — take a vacation in Rome?'

'He is preparing to gather a massive army under the Pope's banner, to journey to Constantinople and beyond. For this he requires money, and King William has offered him ten thousand marks for the right to rule Normandy in his absence.'

'And does King William pledge that, if Duke Robert survives and returns, he will hand Normandy back in due course?'

'That I do not know. I only know that all landholders have been taxed another tithing in order to raise the money.'

'So I have to find one-tenth of the value of my manor, so that one irresponsible ruler may lend money to another?'

'Those are my instructions.'

'Well, here is another one. Leave my estate immediately, unless you wish to leave it tied upside down on your horse.'

The official turned a bright red. 'I will leave as you instruct, but your words will be conveyed to the Earl of Norfolk.'

'I hope so. Tell him also that I might be interested in leasing his lands for nothing, since he did nothing to earn them.'

Some weeks later, Wilfrid looked up from the manorial scrolls he was compiling following the latest harvest returns. Elston was standing hesitantly in the entrance to the small room adjoining the hall in which the manorial records were kept, and he looked distressed.

'What is it?' Wilfrid enquired, concerned by the look on his nephew's face.

'The king has sent men to Ely Abbey, and they are looting it of all its treasures.'

Elston was a regular visitor to Ely, a two-day ride south of Walsingham, since he was hovering on the brink of taking holy orders. His visits had been encouraged by the large congregation of monks established around the abbey by the former Abbot Simeon, who had never been replaced.

'Who has ordered this looting?' Wilfrid enquired.

Elston shrugged. 'It seems that the order came from some man who claims to be the King's Treasurer — "Ranulf" something or other.'

'Ranulf Flambard?'

'Yes, I think that was his name. But the evil work is being conducted by the Earl of Norfolk, in Ranulf's name.'

'And what lawful ground does he have for such an outrage?'

'He claims that the abbey is in debt to King William in return for his consent to the installation of a new abbot following the death of Simeon.'

'But that was several years ago!' Wilfrid protested. 'Was he ever replaced?'

'It would seem not. The monks petitioned the new Archbishop of Canterbury, but it seems that even he has left the country and fled to Normandy because he cannot resolve his differences with the king.'

'Does the earl have any armed men with him?'

'We have not seen the earl himself, only a handful of his ruffians. Presumably he didn't think it would take many men to subdue a few monks.'

Wilfrid rose hastily. 'Seek out Enric, and get him to assemble such men as are available. We'll see if Bigod can be persuaded to leave the abbey empty-handed when he is surrounded by a greater force.'

Wilfrid's contingent of foot soldiers was almost twenty strong as he rode ahead of them through the abbey gates, and gave orders for them to surround the several horse-drawn wagons in the cloister beyond the chapter house. A handful of men were emerging from the abbot's lodging with various gilt items, while two men were struggling out of the quire of the main chapel with a richly painted statue of Christ. Wilfrid gave orders for them to stop what they were doing, and asked to speak to the man who was in charge of 'this wanton act of desecration'.

From out of the chapel strode a fat man with a pockmarked face and a sneering countenance, who looked up at Wilfrid. He was still sitting on his horse.

'What is the meaning of this rude interruption? And who are *you*?'

'Sir Wilfrid de Walsingham, lord of the manor of that name. Who might you be, and what is your authority for this outrage?'

'I carry the authority of the sheriff of this county, Earl Bigod. This abbey is due the Exchequer fifty marks for the right to install a new abbot, and it has thus far failed to pay. We are therefore taking the king's due in kind.'

'Has the new abbot been installed?' Wilfrid demanded.

'None of your business, peasant. Get your men out of here before I advise the sheriff, when he arrives to supervise the removals.'

'He's as corrupt as you,' Wilfrid retorted, 'and my men are here to see that nothing is plundered from this holy house without lawful cause.'

'The lawfulness of the cause is a matter for Sheriff Bigod, and he has already given judgment.'

'The same Roger Bigod who is also Earl of Norfolk?'

'The very same. He also governs Suffolk, and he has ordered this removal.'

'If this removal is as lawful as the demand he made of me for an extra tithe to fund the king's latest quarrel with his brother Robert, then I dispute your authority.'

'That is of course your right and privilege,' the man smiled back triumphantly as he looked out towards the gate entrance, 'and you may exercise both of those immediately, since the sheriff appears to be joining us.'

A long column of heavily armed men mounted on coursers filed through the gate. On a command from the man at their head, they fanned out to surround Wilfrid's smaller, and less well armed, group of foot soldiers from Walsingham. Roger Bigod slipped from his horse and walked over to where the dispute was taking place.

'What's this all about?' he demanded, and his bully lost no time in lodging his complaint.

'This man claims that your ruling regarding the contents of this monastery was without lawful grounds.'

'Does he now?' Bigod replied with raised eyebrows. 'Who might this man be, exactly?'

'Sir Wilfrid de Walsingham, of the estate of that name,' Wilfrid replied defiantly.

Bigod sneered. 'And since when did a Saxon peasant with a pathetic estate consisting of nothing more than a few nuns and a wooden statue of an old lady have greater legal knowledge than a king's sheriff and a Norman earl?'

'The tax that the king claims from this abbey is unlawful,' Wilfrid insisted.

'Just like the tax that you refused to pay for your piddling little estate?' Bigod countered. 'Arrest this traitor!'

As Bigod's men dismounted and drew their swords, Wilfrid's own men formed a protective ring around him and the horse on which he was still mounted, their own few weapons looking embarrassingly inadequate compared with the massive broadswords of the sheriff's men. Wilfrid gave a hasty command for his own men to stand back, and then dismounted in an overt act of submission. He was hastily trussed at the ankles and wrists, and thrown into one of the carts that had been brought to carry away the plunder.

Bigod gave a further order. 'Convey him to Norwich without delay. I'll deal with him on my return.'

X

Wilfrid woke up to yet another day shared with the rats that competed with him for the food, on the rare occasions when it was delivered by a jailor. As for water, Wilfrid dared not drink what was grudgingly tipped into his pail, which looked as if it had just been hauled from the river, since the last thing he needed was an attack of the flux. He'd spent almost a week deep in the dungeons of the castle that he'd once commanded in the king's name. Now, so far as he'd been able to tell from his dim memory of the place and the brief glimpse he'd received while being rolled out of the cart and carried inside, he was somewhere below the Great Hall of Westminster Palace.

There was no window in his airless cell, which was perhaps just as well if they hadn't yet got round to somehow sweetening the Thames that oozed past the palace like a moving privy. Because of that he had no way of telling day from night, other than by the dim light that was visible around the edges of his cell door. He could not even judge the time by his body's need for sleep, since he seemed to spend most of his time in a sort of fitful doze, wondering how Joan and everyone else back at the manor had taken the news of his arrest.

The door opened with its usual grinding screech, and his jailor peered round.

'On yer feet. The king wants ter see yer — let's 'ope 'e don't want ter *smell* yer an' all.'

Wilfrid's arms were shackled on long chains, but he was permitted to walk up two flights of stone spiral stairs, his knees stiff from disuse, until they reached what he took to be the servant's entrance to the Great Hall from the kitchens. Then his feet were also shackled, and he shuffled into the royal presence. He was immediately assailed by a pungent mixture of perfumes that he could only assume came from the various grinning fools who surrounded the king. They were all draped in outrageously long tunics, with jewels on their heeled sandals, and some of them wore ribbons in their hair. As for King William himself, the years of debauchery appeared to be taking their toll, since his face was thinner, and his hair lanker, than Wilfrid remembered it from their last encounter, although this was now some years in the past.

Ranulf Flambard whispered something in William Rufus's ear. The king looked up as Wilfrid was pushed to the floor by his jailor, who hastily retreated to a corner of the room.

The king grinned. 'The high and mighty Lord of Nundom, brought to heel at long last. Are you aware of why you are here, Saxon troublemaker?'

'I assume it's because I defied the Earl of Norfolk in the matter of the extra tithe in taxes.'

'You didn't just defy *him*. In defying him you were defying *me* as well, since he carried my lawful command in his saddlebag. Not content with that, you had the cheek to defy my Treasurer here, since he sought to collect monies lawfully due from the abbey at Ely. Do you deny any of that?'

'I do not deny that I questioned the reason why the dues were being demanded.'

'And why should that concern you, when the money being lawfully demanded at Ely was not even being levied on your manor?'

'I did so to assist those residing at the abbey.'

'Those miserable little men in so-called holy orders, you mean? Those useless lumps who claim to follow an authority higher than mine? If such views are treasonous, is not the behaviour of those who support such traitors in itself treasonous?'

'I simply sought to see the law upheld,' Wilfrid argued, then realised his mistake when Rufus threw the contents of his wine goblet in his direction.

'I am the lawful King of England, and *I* decide what is the law, and what is not, you ungrateful pile of Saxon horse dung! Is that understood?'

'I understand that it is the right of every king to make law that his subjects must follow,' Wilfrid replied tactfully, without conceding anything regarding the moral validity of such laws. This seemed to reduce the regal ire, if not the unhealthy red that had suffused the king's countenance.

'Very well, now that we have that established, tell me why you sent your son to the service of my brother Robert, the pretended Count of Normandy.'

Wilfrid was momentarily taken aback by the extent of the king's information, but he opted for an honest answer. 'He hopes to join the Crusade, to defend the Christian Church.'

William burst into fits of laughter, followed seconds later by those who deemed it diplomatic to join him. 'If the story of that idiot who was stupid enough to open his mouth and get himself silenced by the Romans is to be believed, he only had himself to blame. And those who now claim to follow his lead — are they not themselves Romans? Does whichever Pope is in favour this week not concede that he is the successor to those who did the loud-mouthed troublemaker to death in the first place?'

'That is certainly one view of history,' Wilfrid conceded, appalled by the man's blasphemous profanity.

'It is *my* view of history,' William insisted, 'and therefore *England's* view of history. Why would any sensible ruler these days spend money and men on defending the indefensible and illogical?'

'I believe it's called "The Christian Faith", sire.'

William appeared momentarily pacified by Wilfrid's humble acknowledgment of his royal title, but then his face clouded over once more. 'This woman who claims to have given herself to the Christ myth — she now calls herself "Magdalena", correct?'

'Correct, sire.'

'And before that, she was the widow of Geoffrey de Faverches — a Norman knight who fought with my father, after whom her son is named, yes?'

'Yes, sire.'

'But there are several old men of my court who advise me that before she was bedded by that old goat Faverches, she was the woman of your former Saxon King Harold. Is that something you can confirm?'

'The Mother Magdalena has told me nothing about her past, sire,' Wilfrid lied, 'but it is within my knowledge that before taking the holy veil, her name was "Faverches", and that is the name borne by her son.'

'But you see my point, presumably? If she truly was the widow of Harold of Wessex, then that son of hers who you sent along with your own son, armed with a letter of introduction to my brother in Normandy, could be the next Saxon heir to the English throne, could he not?'

'If your information is correct, then yes — he *could* be,' Wilfrid replied cautiously.

The king's face twisted in anger and disdain. 'And you sent him over to assist my brother, *Saxon?*'

'I sent him over to volunteer for the Crusade, that is all,' Wilfrid insisted.

The king sank into the high back of his throne and smiled unpleasantly. 'I shall be leaving for Normandy within the week. You have to hope, for his sake, that this Geoffrey de Faverches is safely departed for wherever that bunch of fools is scurrying at the whim of this week's Pope, because if he remains within the duchy I shall have him tortured until we get the truth out of him. And if you have played me false in that regard, you will pay for it with your life. Take him away — the smell from him is making me quite ill. He can rot downstairs until my return.'

XI

At approximately the same time that King William was planning his occupation of Normandy, and his search for a possible secret Saxon claimant to the English throne, Geoffrey and Thomas were camped outside the walls of Antioch. They had now learned a few lessons, not just about warfare, but also the treachery inherent in international politics.

After some gruelling training under brutal taskmasters employed in the permanent army of Count Stephen of Blois, in which they had acquitted themselves equally well, the two young men had parted with the faithful horses that had plodded patiently for several weeks through England and northern France. They had been introduced to the far less docile 'destriers' that were bred and trained to carry fully armed knights. They had then been taught how to remain firmly wedged between their high saddle pommels, specially designed to prevent them from being unseated by a lance, and wield a sword half as heavy again as the ones they were used to. Finally, in heavy chainmail covered by the blue and grey livery of the House of Blois, they had ridden out of Blois to a fanfare of trumpets in the lesser ranks of armed knights, well ahead of the combat-grizzled foot soldiers who plodded steadily behind them.

They became part of a much greater army when they met up with the larger force of Robert of Normandy. They were then made even more insignificant once the Normandy and Blois contingents merged under the overall command of Raymond of Toulouse, marching eastward, over mountain ranges and down the shores of shimmering lakes, until a halt was called a few miles short of the glittering towers of Constantinople. There the 'Frankish' army divided into two, and Geoffrey and Thomas, as part of the Blois contingent, were ordered to move into the city proper, while Raymond of Toulouse rode further east to lay siege to Nicaea.

Alexios, Emperor of Byzantium, had hung back from the initial siege of Nicaea, at the end of which the Crusader army under Raymond of Toulouse had made serious inroads into the defending Seljuk army. Then Alexios took command of the remainder of the Crusaders, and Thomas and Geoffrey were among the almost five thousand mounted knights who rode out as part of a Christian force of some thirty thousand.

While the invaders began erecting siege towers, and the defending Seljuk Turks employed miners to burrow under them, Alexios sent emissaries to negotiate the peaceful surrender of Nicaea, then had one of his generals declared the new governor of the city. This new general forbade any looting or mass entry into the conquered city, and the thousands of frustrated Crusaders who had been anticipating a reward for the risks they had been taking marched further east, proclaiming their intention of capturing Jerusalem. Four months later they had reached Antioch, and it was there that this First Crusade ground to a halt.

During the eight months in which Antioch was under siege from the Crusader army, serious rifts appeared in its leadership. The Northern Franks, who included Stephen of Blois, were becoming suspicious of the long-term territorial ambitions of the main French force under Raymond of Toulouse, a Southern Frank. It needed only an outbreak of the Plague, and a devastating shortage of fresh food that forced parts of the Christian host to cannibalise the dead bodies of their fallen enemies, to convince Stephen that he would be better employed defending his own territory between Orleans and Tours, given the reports he was receiving regarding the activities of William of England and his younger brother Henry. He therefore ordered a general retreat back west, and Thomas and Geoffrey were content to obey, given the appalling conditions under which they had been forced to live for the past few months. They left Count Robert to continue to stare at the walls of Antioch.

Neither Thomas nor Geoffrey had 'enjoyed' any opportunity to display their prowess in open battle, and both of them were therefore still squires in the immediate service of Count Stephen of Blois. Squires or not, they had attracted many a lascivious glance from the ladies of the Court of Blois. While Geoffrey celebrated that fact by engaging in activities with high-born ladies of which his abbess mother would have heartily disapproved, Thomas proved more discerning. But even he, as a healthy and physically active young man approaching his twenty-second year, was not immune from bodily urges that seemed to almost overpower him when he was in the company of a certain woman. Her name was Emma, and she had a fresh complexion, long dark hair and a voluptuous figure.

She was a regular presence at the Court of Blois, and Count Stephen seemed to regard her with great affection, despite the disapproving glares that she received from the Countess Adela whenever she was present. The popular rumour was that she was the bastard daughter of Stephen himself, the product of one of his many affairs, this one with a princess from Aquitaine, to the south of Blois. Emma was certainly different in appearance from the acknowledged daughters of Blois, Lucia, Agnes and Eleanor, all of whom had inherited their mother's distinctive red-gold locks and diminutive figure. Once

Geoffrey and Thomas had been presented at court, with a letter of recommendation from Robert of Normandy, Emma had taken immediately to the tall, handsome, red-haired visitor from England with the spare, muscular frame and the elegant French that was lacking in his more blunt-faced and awkward companion.

Emma seemed to enjoy more freedom than her alleged stepsisters, and rumour had it that she was free with her favours around the more prominent older men of the Court of Blois, among whom she appeared to be seeking a match. Countess Adela had more than once complained to her husband that 'the girl Emma' was a bad influence among the more demure ladies of the court, but Count Stephen, as usual, had ignored complaints regarding her behaviour, further confirming the suggestion that she was his daughter.

The Crusaders had only been back in Blois for a few days when Emma entered the stables in which Thomas was supervising the shoeing of his war horse. She was leading her own grey mare by its bridle.

'I think my mare Isabella may be lame in one of her hind legs,' Emma purred. 'Could you take a look at her?'

'I am no farrier, madam,' Thomas assured her as he breathed in her heavy perfume, 'and I would not know what to look for.'

'Would you know what to look for in a woman?' Emma asked.

'I think so,' Thomas replied huskily as his throat suddenly went dry.

'And would you like to see more of this one?' she enquired.

'Without a doubt,' Thomas croaked.

'My chamber is in the east tower, on the second floor,' she advised him in a more business-like tone. 'I shall dismiss my attendants after supper has been served in the main hall, and you may conduct your inspection then.'

After several months of the clandestine entwining of bodies, Thomas didn't care if Emma was free with her favours. She was his on a nightly basis, and he had never known such bliss. He guiltily wondered what his parents might say, were they to find out how he had lost his virginity to a young beauty who, he suspected, had her own motives for lying with him. He persuaded himself that it was only his body she craved, and not some hope of social advancement. After all, he reasoned, he was only a lowly squire, so what could he offer her other than carnal pleasure?

Then came word that all the fighting men who owed allegiance to Count Stephen were required to journey north to the fortress of Alencon. Technically it was part of the Duchy of Normandy, and therefore within the suzerainty of Count Robert, but before embarking on the ill-fated Crusade he had allowed his land to be governed by his treacherous brother William, who was now giving every indication that he never intended to hand it back. William claimed that he was defending the Duchy from hostile neighbours in Vexin, to the south, to whom Robert had always shown the face of weakness and indecision.

He was aided in this by their younger brother Henry, who, even though he had now reached manhood, was still obviously in the thrall of his older, fiercer brother. In return for three thousand marks given to Robert as further funding for his crusading ambitions, Henry had been granted an area known as the Cotentin, to the north of Blois and to the west of Normandy. From here he had command of several Channel ports such as Cherbourg, and was well positioned to reinforce any army he cared to recruit from England in order to march south against his brother-in-law Stephen. Left to his own devices, it was unlikely that he would attempt anything so warlike and aggressive, but as usual he feared King William of England who, while reinforcing his grip on Normandy, was said to be recruiting in England for a supplementary force to cross Cotentin and enter Blois. Alencon was the strongest fortress between the two, and Stephen of Blois decided, as a matter of caution, to swell its garrison against any encroachment south from Cotentin.

Both Thomas and Geoffrey were summoned to arms. As Thomas bid a temporary farewell to Emma on their final night together for some time, she kissed him gently on the mouth and whispered, 'Take good care to avoid death or serious injury while you are away. I want your body back here in one piece, and the child that I believe to be in my womb requires a father.'

Thomas stared back at her. 'Are you sure?' he enquired, open-mouthed.

'Sure I am with child, or sure that it's yours?' Emma replied. 'I am well aware how I am perceived by the woman who will not acknowledge me as a stepdaughter, but you are the only one I've lain with these many weeks past. It's yours, dearest Thomas, and I love you. So come back in one piece.'

For the entire five-day ride to Alencon, Thomas was like a man transfixed. Geoffrey, riding alongside him, was well aware of Thomas's nightly trysts with the Lady Emma, and put down his white-faced silence to his regret at having to leave her. He made a vow to himself that no woman would ever take over his conscious will, and possibly his wits, in the same way that Thomas appeared to have been bewitched.

They reached Alencon to be greeted by the news that William was heading south-west to challenge Stephen's right to defend Alencon, which was part of Normandy, even against Henry, who was thought to be in Caen with English reinforcements. But Stephen defied him, convinced that William's Norman force was planning to combine with English reinforcements given safe passage through the Cotentin by his brother Henry, in order to mount a combined attack on Blois.

Lookouts were stationed on the town walls, and the gates of the town were securely locked at nightfall every day. Count Stephen took up residence in the mayor's mansion, surrounded by men at arms who took it in turn to guard their lord as he slept. During this period of uncertainty, there were many desertions by men at arms who were unsure as to which of the sons of William the Bastard they owed allegiance, and Stephen made those who guarded his person renew their oaths of allegiance every day when they came on duty.

Unknown to any of them, one of the deserters, Hugh de Saint-Sulpice, saw an opportunity to acquire some wealth with which to inject new life into his failing vineyard estate. He rode hard to the east and encountered King William's advancing army at Dreux, where it had camped overnight because the men were too exhausted to journey further west on the forced march towards Alencon. Hugh sought an audience with William, who was summoned from his bed to be advised that the man who had just arrived from Alencon knew a place where its walls had been weakened by local townsfolk removing the stonework for their own houses, and this section had not yet been reinforced by Count Stephen. Hugh earned enough money to allow him to return home rejoicing. William summoned his strongest and boldest knights and ordered them to test the stamina of their coursers by racing to Alencon to take immediate advantage of the weakness of its town's defences.

Thomas was on guard duty outside Count Stephen's bedchamber when he heard a commotion from the street outside. Drawing his broadsword, he quickly moved to the staircase down which the main door was accessed, in time to hear screams and curses as the heavy front door crashed open. A dozen heavily armed men rushed through, hacking the door guards to the floor and racing up the stairs. Thomas slipped back, and waited until the sounds of heavy tramping, and the creaking of chainmail, betrayed the fact that the intruders were almost at the top of the stairs, then he leaped out, swinging his double-edge blade with all his might.

To his delight, three heads lifted from their necks and bounced along the carpet, forcing the remaining invaders to either step round the dead torsos of their fallen companions, or leap over them. Thomas was ready as they came at him individually, and he was able to put paid to two more of them with wild, slashing strokes before reinforcements piled up the stairs from behind, and four more men wearing the livery of England hit the carpet with a squelching thud.

The one remaining intruder turned, as if to run back, then hesitated when he saw that his path to the staircase was blocked by defenders. He turned and lunged wildly at Thomas, who fended off the attack by blocking it with his sword, then with all his remaining strength he gave an upward thrust that threw his assailant's sword clean out of his hand and up towards the low ceiling. With a grin of triumph Thomas rammed his sword into the vulnerable gap in the chainmail under the man's armpit, while his arms were still in the air, then as he screamed in pain and doubled forward, Thomas sliced off his fourth head of the evening, then doubled over to regain his breath.

As he came back upright, he saw that the defenders who had come up the staircase, and were facing down the corridor with wide eyes, had dropped to their knees. Thomas looked behind him, and there in the doorway to the bedroom was Count Stephen, still in his night shirt, with a broad smile on his face.

'This calls for wine,' he announced. 'And find someone to clean up that mess.'

Two days later, Thomas was awakened from an uneasy afternoon slumber in his barrack room by the noise of men hastily donning their armour. From somewhere outside a herald was blowing the general call to arms, and Thomas hastily climbed into his chainmail, grabbed his sword and shield and raced to the north town wall. He looked over the parapet to the sight of a sizeable army wending its way out of the distant Forêt d'Écouves, and he began tightening his chain leathers in anticipation of the opening salvo in a siege. Then the man next to him let out a chuckle.

'They look as if they want to parley.'

A man carrying a battle standard adorned with English lions in one hand, and a flagpole bearing a plain white pennant in the other, had ridden out from the front line of William's forces, which had meanwhile come to a halt. As the emissary trotted closer to the town walls, a call came down the line for 'Thomas Walsingham' to report, with his horse, in front of the mayor's house. He did so, and found himself part of a small escort, the rest of whom were all knights exercising their destriers in wide circles over the cobbles as they awaited their commander. Count Stephen duly appeared on the steps, and a groom brought round his horse, decked from ears to tail in heraldic drapes of gaudy hue, like some sort of travelling sideshow attraction.

Stephen was assisted onto his horse, and called for Thomas to ride by his side.

'Why me, my Lord?' Thomas enquired.

Stephen smiled across at him as they trotted two abreast through the north gate. 'To judge by your exploits two nights ago, you are the finest bodyguard I have in my service. Not that I expect any treachery — my guess is that William now simply seeks safe passage through to Cotentin, where his brother Henry awaits him.'

'But then they may combine their forces and attack Alencon, may they not?'

'They may indeed, but by then we will have fallen back on Blois, where we have a heavily fortified chateau in which to defend ourselves. I intend to send you and your friend de Faverches back to the Holy Land, to warn Count Robert what his brother is about in Normandy. Why should I waste men and horses defending his possessions while he adds to his favour with God?'

An hour later, they had completed the largely formal process of exchanging pleasantries with the emissary sent ahead by King William, and had given a pledge to take no aggressive action for as long as the English force kept going, and turned north into Cotentin. For some reason, William had decided against taking on Stephen's army, and it was rumoured that it was to do with his own ill health; it was even rumoured that once in Cotentin, he would take ship from Cherbourg back to the south coast of England at Lymington.

As they trotted easily back towards the town side by side, Count Stephen turned to look at Thomas. 'You came to my court seeking an opportunity to obtain your knighthood in the

Holy Land, but now you seem reluctant to re-engage in that ambition. I believe I know the reason for that.'

'My lord?'

'A certain lady who is bearing your child?'

Thomas could not find the words to reply, but Stephen was in an expansive mood.

'You need not fear my wrath by admitting it, but the lady of your affections *is* with child, is she not?'

'So she informs me, my lord.'

'And you are aware of who she is?'

'I know only of the rumour, my lord,' Thomas replied as he prayed for the earth to consume both him and his horse.

Stephen chuckled. 'Let us not mince words, Thomas. I would be delighted to have a grandchild by such a strong and fearless warrior. But you cannot think in terms of marriage — even an illegitimate daughter of mine must be expected to look higher.'

'I love her, my lord.'

'I should hope so, for if I thought for one moment that you had merely used her body, I would take your head from your shoulders. But you may at least draw some comfort from what is to follow this evening after supper.'

'My lord?'

'The father of my grandchild will become *Sir* Thomas Walsingham, by my hand. Then I want you back in the Holy Land, where your no doubt jealous English companion with the French name must strive to match your elevation.'

XII

The entire convent was grouped around the statue of the Virgin, deep in prayer, accompanied by Joan and Elston. Mother Magdalena led the tearful pleas to the Blessed Mother to look down mercifully on their offspring Thomas and Geoffrey, and to send comfort and succour to Wilfrid in his hour of greatest need.

It had been many months since Enric had raced back to Walsingham with the news that Wilfrid had been detained by Earl Bigod, and then transported down to London, where he was believed to be in a dungeon below the Palace of Westminster. Joan was a tearful wreck as she went about her daily household chores, while Matilda had worked her way through her rosary so many times that her voice had become a husky rasp. Elston had promised God that if he would intercede on his uncle's behalf, he would spend the rest of his days in His service, and the entire estate behaved as if in deep mourning.

Magdalena ended the formal prayers, and looked up to the statue one final time. 'Dearest lady, you lost your only son through the cruelty of those who abused their power. For the love you bear for all humanity, bring succour and comfort to our brother Wilfrid as he bravely bears the insults and indignities inflicted on him by those who know not what they do, or why they do it. Amen.'

Over a hundred miles to the south, Wilfrid had almost lost awareness of who he was, or why he was there. Months and months of solitary confinement in a stinking cell a few feet square, with only slits of light around his cell door to tell him whether it was day or night, had slowly caused his memories to seep into his reality, until reality faded into timeless nothing. Had he been placed here because he had offended the thegn by not grinding his corn finely enough? Or had he died on the battlefield near his home in a village whose name now escaped him, and was he in Hell? But, then again, wasn't there a beautiful woman somewhere, and didn't he once used to play with a pretty little girl and a mischievous boy who looked like him? It was all a swirling confusion that came and went, but he remembered a statue somewhere of a lady who was very important.

Wilfrid's eyes were attracted to a shadow on the wall that grew more distinct as he stared at it. The dim image of a face became more detailed, and then the colour began to fall into place, beginning with the peaceful eyes, the colour of the morning sky over the sea, then the flawless complexion, and the hint of a dimpled smile as the face came to life. He felt the emotions rising within him, as he heard the gentle words: 'Have faith and be comforted.'

Then the vision faded, and he collapsed in tears of despair as all the memories flooded back to him. He had remembered why he was there, and he could never hope to be released.

After what must have been several more days, the cell door opened with its usual grating reluctance, and there in the doorway stood a tall monk, a shadow against the light that seemed so bright after all the gloom to which he was accustomed.

'Uncle Wilfrid?' the monk enquired, and suddenly Wilfrid remembered that he had family.

'Selwyn?' he enquired in his confusion.

'No, Elston. Selwyn's son. "Brother Mark" now, as you can see.' He stepped towards Wilfrid, who backed away in alarm.

'No, don't embrace me — I smell disgusting. What of your mother? Sorry, I mean your aunt. And your mother, of course — isn't she my sister?'

'My mother continues to thrive as Sister Grace, and now has ten novitiates under her care, as well as an orphanage of seven children to care for. Your wife Joan — my aunt — prays daily for your release and return, and your daughter Matilda has proved herself a tower of strength in running both your manor and her school. They will sing praises to God to know that you are still alive.'

'For all the use I am to them,' Wilfrid replied, on the verge of tears. 'How long have I been here?'

'It's been over a year,' Elston advised him. 'The king was in Normandy for most of that time, and probably forgot that you were here, but I shall remind him on his return, even if he takes my head for it.'

'He may take mine, if he remembers I'm here,' Wilfrid replied ruefully. 'But perhaps I would welcome it.'

'Let us say a prayer together, Uncle,' Elston urged him. He knelt by the door, which was still open, although the guard was maintaining a careful vigil a few feet down the corridor.

The prayer finished, and Elston rose to his feet, leaving Wilfrid still on his knees.

'Can you still stand, Uncle?' he enquired.

'I can, but I am so weak that I prefer to sit. The Virgin visited my cell a few days ago. Or was it weeks? Some time ago, anyway. She told me to be of good cheer, and then you arrive. Am I dreaming this? I do dream, I believe, although it's sometimes difficult to know the difference.'

'We gathered round the shrine and prayed for your deliverance,' Elston advised him. 'That must have been what moved her to compassion.'

'Thank you for that,' Wilfrid whispered. 'When you return, thank everyone for their love and concern. Tell your mother that she's a good sister. Tell Tilly I'm proud of her. Tell your aunt…'

He broke down and sobbed, thumping his fists on the damp floor of the cell. Elston looked down in pity and compassion as he made the sign of the cross.

'I'll carry all those messages faithfully, Uncle, but now I have to go. The jailor was bribed for only a short while, and even that would not have been possible had the king been in residence.'

'Where is he? Still in Normandy?'

'He returned from there recently, in the company of his brother Henry, or so I'm informed. He now holds court at Winchester, and has declared his intention of going hunting. I have never wished evil on a man before, but were he to die…'

'Elston,' Wilfrid replied in a warning voice.

Elston sighed. 'How can you be so forgiving in your heart, after what William has done to you?'

Wilfrid gave a small, ironic laugh. '*You* are the clergyman in the family, and the son of a nun. Have you not yet learned that retribution is the preserve of God, if the holy books are to be believed? We men must meekly accept what Fate deals out to us.'

The three weeks that followed seemed no more than another passing day in Wilfrid's mind-numbing routine. He didn't even bother to look up when the cell door ground open again.

'Yer lucky charm musta worked,' said the jailor. 'Yer free ter go, an' I've ter tek yer upstairs fer a dousin' under the pump in the yard. Then yer've ter be fitted out wiv new clothes, an' fed.'

Wilfrid looked up at him blankly. 'Free to go, you say?'

'That's it, yer daft lump. Free as a little dicky bird.'

'King William's ordered my release?'

'No, not 'im — 'is brother. William's dead, and 'Enry's the king now.'

XIII

If it was a dream, then it was the best he had enjoyed for some time, Wilfrid concluded as he gazed down at the plate of fish that had just been laid in front of him. The serving girl slipped quietly out of the small but well-appointed chamber to which he had been led by an usher, and in which he had found a new green tunic and brown hose laid out on the first bed he had seen since he had been arrested.

Wilfrid reached up and gingerly fingered his slightly cut face, now clean shaven after a barber had, somewhat clumsily, carved off his long grey beard. That much, at least, was real. He also smelt better than he could ever remember, but just in case the cold water and rough stone that had removed most of the prison grime had not been sufficient to erase the odour of lengthy captivity, there was a selection of oils and unguents on a side table. When he was advised what was next in store for him, he would decide whether or not to make use of them.

The door to the chamber opened wide, and there stood the same liveried usher who had shown him to the chamber.

'When you have finished eating, the king wishes to see you.'

Wilfrid dropped the knife hastily, and cleared his mouth of the portion of fish he had been savouring. He took a mouthful of the small beer that had also been provided, and smiled. 'Surely, a king should not be kept waiting while one of his subjects eats?'

'He has several others to see,' the usher advised him, 'since he has released most of those who were confined below. Simply come into the hallway when you are finished, and I will place you in the list.'

99

A few minutes later, replete with the largest meal he had consumed for at least the past year, and suitably oiled and perfumed, Wilfrid presented himself in the long carpeted corridor outside, and was led up several flights of stairs that somehow seemed familiar. Then his returning memory supplied the answer — it was an access stairway to the royal chambers, which he had used several times when he'd served as a housecarl to King Harold Godwinson. That now seemed like a life that someone else had led.

After a moderate wait outside a set of heavy double oak doors, one of them opened to reveal the face of another royal usher, this one finely dressed in a tunic that bore on its chest the heraldic lions of England.

'Wilfrid Walsingham?' he was asked, and he nodded. The door was opened wider, and the jerk of the usher's head indicated for him to enter. He walked in as erect and proud as his still stiffened limbs permitted, and there, sitting on a throne at the end of the long gallery, sat the man who had presumably liberated him.

Henry of England had grown into a man in the years since Wilfrid had last seen him. But beneath the shock of black hair there was a barrel chest and a considerable gut, betraying the fact that however Henry had spent his formative years, it had not been in healthy exercise.

The king beckoned him forward, and Wilfrid bowed the knee when still several paces from the throne, then looked up with a smile. He was met with a quizzical look.

'You are much changed in appearance, unless my memory plays me false,' Henry observed. 'I remember a sturdy man who was more than a match for my struggling older brother when he held him by the seat of his hose. Do I address the same man?'

'Indeed you do, sire, and one who owes you his eternal gratitude for the mercy you have shown me in ordering my release.'

'You should never have been confined in the first place, and neither should those I released at the same time, some of whom regrettably appear to have lost their wits from the experience. You, I suspect, have merely lost weight.'

'Indeed, sire. I have dined at better tables than that supplied by the royal jailor.'

Henry chuckled. 'You have even retained a sense of humour, it would seem. How old are you now?'

'What year is it, sire?'

Henry's jaw dropped. 'For the love of God, how long were you confined down there?'

'I have no way of knowing, sire, hence my request that you advise me of the date.'

'It is late August in the year 1100. Does that help?'

Wilfrid thought for a moment, then nodded. 'Indeed, sire. I believe that I am now fifty-two.'

'You have a wife and family?'

'So I believe, sire. A wife and daughter in Walsingham, where I am — or perhaps I should say *was* — the lord of the manor. I also have a son who I last saw when he rode off to join your brother Robert's Crusader army. I have heard nothing of him since, and he may well be dead, for all I know.'

'It is to be hoped that Robert commands his men with more skill than he governs Normandy, certainly. But do you not have a son who has taken holy orders?'

'A nephew, certainly. He visited me recently, while I was still confined, although it was in secret. I hope he will not be punished for that?'

'Why should he be, when he was the means of your release? A persistent monk who seemed destined to haunt me wherever I went, until I finally agreed to hear his petition. It was he who reminded me of the day you saved me from the wicked Rufus — it seems that you told the tale often around your family.'

'Indeed, sire, if you will forgive me. We meant no dishonour to you, but during those dark days when we were oppressed by the former king, it was a source of considerable comfort to be reminded that he had once been an errant youth berated by his father.'

Henry smiled. 'Our father was a very powerful man in his day, but he showed little wisdom when he left England to the favourite son. The nation I have inherited has suffered grievously at Rufus's hands, but it is my intention to put right the wrongs of former years. Beginning, of course, with the release of those who defied him.'

'I did not defy him, sire, since I respect the authority of a king, whoever he may be. I simply sought justice.'

'It may well be,' Henry replied with an even broader smile, 'that we can find a worthy cause for that love of truth that you claim for yourself. In particular, I have need of a man whose honesty is above reproach, in order to clear my name of a grievous accusation.'

'If I might be permitted to journey home first, sire…'

'Yes, yes, of course. I shall instruct that you be given a horse, and a purse of money. Take your leave whenever you feel strong enough, but I trust you to return in due course and be of particular service to me, in a matter that affects the security of my crown.'

'Gladly, sire.'

'Good. Well, I must not delay you any longer, although this brief audience must have seemed to you a mere flutter of an eyelid, given the time that you spent languishing below here. You may withdraw.'

Wilfrid approached the entrance to Walsingham Manor with his heart in his mouth. He'd been away for so long, and he was unsure what sort of welcome he would receive. Immediate joy, with hugs and kisses, no doubt, but later…? Joan had, prior to his imprisonment, been swift to complain loudly about his frequent absences. Only his own rash stupidity could be blamed for this latest one, which by Wilfrid's calculation had lasted for well over a year and a half. He knew they had been praying for him, and Elston had reassured him that the manor had at least survived, if not prospered, under Matilda's careful management. To judge by the crops he could see in the fields leading down to, and across, the river than ran through the estate, it would be a good harvest this year, but what did his tenants think of a lord who was missing so often, and for so long?

Ahead of him, seated on the bench outside the manor house door, he could see a slightly built woman with white hair. At first he took her to be Mother Magdalena. Then he reminded himself that the lady in question was never seen other than in her holy vestments, and certainly not in the bright blue, if somewhat dog-eared, gown in the style and colour that he remembered Joan wearing. Then the realisation hit him, and with a large lump rising in his throat he dismounted and led the horse through the gate.

Joan looked up resignedly as she anticipated yet another disappointment. She'd been advised by a joyful Elston that Wilfrid had been released by the new king, but every man who had ridden through the gate during the past weeks had raised her heartbeat, only to plunge her into another pit of despair when he turned out to be a tradesman or an itinerant pedlar.

This was a thin, middle-aged man, whoever he was, and not the robust warrior in the prime of life who had set off to preserve the treasures of Ely Abbey, and had never returned. Joan stood up, preparing to welcome the visitor with as much politeness as she could muster from her deflated spirit, then she wondered why he was grinning stupidly at her. Did she know him? The eyes looked familiar as he grew closer, and that boyish grin she'd known for years. Then he called her name and opened his arms, and she dropped to the ground in a dead faint.

'She'll come round in a moment, Wilfrid,' Magdalena reassured him.

Wilfrid looked down forlornly at his wife, who they'd carried to her bed. Matilda had heard his cry of alarm from just inside the orphanage, where she'd been lining the children up for their midday walk, and she had rushed out, tears flowing down her cheeks, to throw herself at her weeping father. She'd then turned her attention to her mother. Sister Grace had summoned Magdalena, and she in turn had summoned the now elderly Merrys Winterborn, despite her misgivings regarding 'natural physick', as the wisewoman called it.

Merrys wafted the burning herbs under Joan's nose. Her eyes flew open, taking in the circle of heads that surrounded her as they looked down solemnly. Her husband's tears were now dripping onto her gown as he leaned in and kissed her burning forehead.

'Will, is that *really* you?' she whispered, and he nodded.

'God be praised,' Sister Grace mumbled, while Mother Magdalena preferred to discharge herself of a long stream of Latin. Merrys Winterborn backed away respectfully and stepped out of the room with a smile, then everyone began talking at once.

'I thought I'd never see you again,' Joan sobbed later that night, as Wilfrid held her tightly to his chest and gazed at the ceiling above them, sending a silent prayer to the Blessed Virgin. He vowed to encase her shrine in gold once he had the means to do so.

'Well, I'm back, and the nation seems to be in better hands, if my first encounter with our new king's anything to go by.'

'What's he like?' Joan enquired as she wiped her eyes yet again.

'To look at, or in his manner?' Wilfrid enquired.

Joan snorted. 'Now I *know* it's really you — always the stupid questions. Who cares what he looks like? How does he conduct himself?'

'Mercifully, and justly, as my release demonstrates. But he's asked for my help.'

'No!' Joan yelled, then bit her lip in the hope that she hadn't awakened the entire household. 'You promised! And you've already broken that promise, and got yourself locked up for almost two years. You may be a good fighter, Will Riveracre, but you're not fit to be allowed out without someone like me to keep your mouth guarded.'

Wilfrid chuckled. '"Will Riveracre". It's been many a year since I was called that.'

'Well, that's who you were born, that's who you were when we first met, and that's who you'll always be, deep down. A miller's son with a gift for getting himself involved with kings, and always to his disadvantage.'

'I was knighted by one king,' Wilfrid reminded her.

'And imprisoned by the next,' Joan retorted. 'What will this next one do to you — get you with child?'

Wilfrid chuckled again. 'Talking of children, how old's Tilly now?'

'Thirty-three, and far too old for you to marry her off to some doddery old earl, if that's what you promised the new king.'

'No, but I *did* promise — and please don't get angry, since I'm only just home again — but I did promise that I'd return to court and help him with some legal problem or other.'

'You're not a lawyer.'

'No, but he seems to have regard for my reputation for honesty. Allow me that, at least.'

'Well, you're not going without me this time,' Joan insisted.

'I have no intention of doing, believe me,' Wilfrid assured her. 'All that time in that stinking cell, I thought about how much I missed you. Your smile, your cooking, your advice — even your scolding.'

'I *don't* scold!' Joan insisted.

'Oh yes you do, and I love you for it,' Wilfrid laughed lightly.

It fell silent for a moment, then Joan asked quietly, 'Is that all you remembered about me?'

'Was there something I left out?'

'No more than usual. What about my tempting body, which at one time you couldn't keep your hands off?'

'Oh yes, I remembered those early days too.'

106

'Not just early days,' Joan reminded him. 'Were there not times, when you were lying there, that you wished I was lying next to you?'

'Yes, of course, why?'

'Well, I'm lying next to you now.'

'You mean…?'

'What do you think I mean? Or do you need a plan written on vellum?'

'Of course not. It's just that … well, it's been so long.'

'Then let me remind you.'

XIV

Thomas guided his horse reluctantly down the ramp from the vessel that had brought them, along with many hundreds of others, back down the Black Sea from Constantinople. Thomas was no sailor, and even though the vast stretch of water on which they'd spent the past three days was classed as an inland sea, the gale force winds had whipped up waves sufficiently high to engender seasickness in the men and fear in their horses. They were headed for Nicomedia, and Thomas was still trying to understand why.

The news had echoed all around Europe the previous year that the Crusaders who'd pressed on after an exhausting, but successful, siege of Antioch had eventually overrun Jerusalem, and had installed a western king. The first of them had died within the first year, but now Baldwin of Boulogne reigned supreme over the ancient birthplace of Christianity, so why were reinforcements needed? And why had Stephen of Blois decided to join them?

To those with a wider grasp of the facts, it was difficult to know which of two possible alternatives had prevailed. On the one hand, Stephen could have been shamed into it by the new Pope Paschal II, who urged those who had either not joined the original Crusade at all, or who had turned back at Antioch, to swell the numbers commanding the Holy City. Alternatively, it could have been the scornful jibes of Stephen's wife Adela, who said that he had not been courageous enough to engage a real enemy, and had merely stirred the pot from the sidelines as her Norman brothers bickered among themselves.

To explain the need for their second journey east, Stephen had told Thomas that they had to warn Robert of Normandy that his youngest brother Henry had lost no time in claiming the throne of England following the death of their brother William Rufus. But Thomas was at a loss to understand why that should be of such importance to Stephen that he needed to march back into inhospitable terrain. Robert was said to be in Jerusalem, with which there was regular communication, so why not simply dispatch a messenger?

Thomas's displeasure at being called to arms as part of his newly won knighthood was not abated by the fact that the departure had been less than a week after their return from Alencon, during which time he had been strictly forbidden to have anything to do with the Lady Emma, who was not in any case visible at court any longer. Countess Adela had let it be believed that Emma had been sent back to her native Aquitaine for the sake of her health, but Thomas suspected that it was more a matter of suppressing gossip about her condition.

While Thomas was displeased at being where they were, his companion Geoffrey de Faverches was only too anxious to earn his spurs in battle. It rankled with him that Thomas had been knighted first, when, in his opinion, he was the better fighter.

By the time they reached Nicomedia, they had joined forces with other western retinues, most notably those of the Burgundy princes and the Holy Roman Emperor, the German Henry IV. Henry had, seemingly under his command, the now almost legendary Raymond of Toulouse, who had made the capture of Jerusalem possible on the first occasion. But they were no more a cohesive army under unanimous leadership than they had ever been, and the Crusader camp in reality consisted of clusters of tents in which those of the same nationality kept strictly to themselves.

They even fought in different ways, under different leaders, and occasionally at different times. The Turkish leaders took full advantage of both that and the terrain that suited their tactics of swift horse-borne attacks on Crusader camps. It was the last of these, at Mersivan, that sent the westerners scattering in all directions, leaving weapons, supplies, and even camp followers behind in their desperation to make it to the safety of the vessels they had left moored ready for a hasty return to Constantinople.

By the time that they rode back into Blois, Geoffrey de Faverches was no nearer to realising his ambition to become a knight, and almost a year had passed. He angrily announced his intention of returning to Walsingham, and challenged Thomas to accompany him. He believed that in England Thomas's knighthood would not be recognised, and they would be back on an equal footing. Thomas was still undecided about whether he wanted to return to what would almost certainly be a demand from his ageing father that he take on more of the burden of running the estate, but one day his mind was made up for him.

He was sitting in the guardhouse of the castle, sharpening his sword and waiting for his horse to be re-shod, when a message was delivered to him by a page who seemed eager to scuttle away. It was very brief, and contained only a location — the main stables — and a time, after supper that evening. Since this had been his regular assignation time with Emma, his hopes rose, and he was at the stables well before the supper trestles in the main hall had been dismantled.

Thomas became alert when there was a furtive movement to one side of him. A young maid emerged from the shadows, dressed in dark clothing and carrying a bundle.

'Sir Thomas Walsingham?' she enquired conspiratorially, and Thomas whispered his confirmation. The woman handed him the bundle, which was warm and soft, and stirring slightly. He opened the wrapping, and inside was a baby that was only weeks old, to judge by the fuzzy dark hair on its scalp, the softness of the skull when Thomas stroked it, and the almost mole-like eyes.

'It's beautiful,' Thomas murmured, 'but why…'

'Your daughter,' the woman replied urgently. 'My lady Emma wishes you to take her to England and raise her as your own.'

'I cannot take responsibility for a small infant such as this,' Thomas protested. 'She needs her mother.'

'I did not mean this very night,' the woman assured him. 'But when she is no longer so feeble, you will take her to England?'

'I will return to England and make the arrangements,' Thomas promised. He leaned down, gave the stirring infant a gentle kiss, then handed her back. 'Tell your mistress that I still love her, and that I will return.'

'My mistress told me to pledge to you her undying love also,' the woman smiled back. 'She says to tell you that she will find some way of journeying to England to be with you.'

XV

Wilfrid spent the first week or so after his return catching up with all that been happening while he had been a prisoner. From Tilly he learned that girls were not as useless in the management of estates as tradition would have it, and he gratefully accepted the scrolls that recorded two ample harvests, an increase in the rental roll and the birth of several promising-looking foals to the two brood mares.

'I had expected to have to leave all this to Thomas,' Wilfrid smiled at Tilly. 'Is there any news of his likely return? Your mother said that a letter came from somewhere in France announcing that he had been knighted.'

'That was last year,' Tilly frowned, 'and we have heard nothing since. But Mother Magdalena hears from Geoffrey more often, and it seems that they are headed back to the Holy Land. She is pleased, as the abbess of a convent, but worried as a mother.'

'As indeed she has every right to be,' Wilfrid conceded. 'But what of you, Matilda of Walsingham? Do you have suitors?'

'Only spotty estate youths who want to fondle my curves, or perhaps impregnate me with their seed. They are all ugly and unrefined, and the only man with anything to command a woman's interest is Enric's son Ralph, who now conducts the training of the village men in the use of arms. But he is betrothed to Edith Broad, the weaver's daughter.'

'Do you not wish for a husband?'

'Not from among the local men, certainly. Mother says that you will be returning to court — may I come with you?'

'And what of the orphanage and school?'

'One of the village girls — Freda — shows great promise as both a nurse and a teacher. If we have any serious illness, there is always Elston — "Brother Mark" as he is now — who is in holy orders at Ely Abbey. He works alongside the infirmarian there, learning how to tend the sick.'

'I must journey to Ely, to thank Elston properly for securing my release.'

'You should also thank the Holy Virgin,' Sister Grace insisted as she swept in carrying a bundle of clothing that had been washed by her novitiates as part of their divine duties.

Wilfrid allowed himself a chuckle. 'Trust my own sister to put me in my place. I must consult with Mother Magdalena regarding the vision I had of the Virgin during the lowest time of my confinement, just before Elston came to see me.'

'We held a prayer vigil, to plead with the Holy Virgin for her intervention to ensure your comfort and deliverance,' Elva advised him. 'That was not the first miracle she has performed, and if we witness any more we intend to communicate them to Rome.'

Three weeks after his return, Wilfrid became aware of a minor commotion at the manor entrance. Many of the voices being raised were male, and, fearing that someone such as Earl Bigod was intent on plunder during the believed absence of the lord of the manor, Wilfrid walked hastily outside. A man was climbing down from his horse, surrounded by well-wishers. As Wilfrid walked towards the new arrival, Mother Magdalena raced past him, her black robes fluttering behind her, and embraced the man. With a sinking heart, Wilfrid followed behind her and looked hard into Geoffrey's eyes as he stared at him over his mother's shoulder.

'Thomas?' Wilfrid enquired, his heart in his mouth.

Geoffrey smiled back reassuringly. 'He's still in London somewhere. I left him there not three days ago.'

'Why did he choose not to return with you?'

Geoffrey shrugged. 'He would not say. He was very secretive all the time while we were crossing the Channel from Cherbourg, but I believe that there is a woman involved. He was very close with one of Count Stephen's daughters.'

'How went matters in the Holy Land?' Magdalena enquired as she took her son's arm and steered him back towards the manor house, Wilfrid walking alongside them.

'Very confused, and the outcome uncertain. The Crusade leaders seem more intent on arguing among themselves, and we were badly led. Twice we had to retreat in a great hurry, and I was lucky to escape with my life. Many did not.'

'But Thomas is safe, you say?' Wilfrid asked again.

'Safe from slaughter, but I fear that this woman of whom I spoke has him in her clutches.'

'Why do you fear it?'

'Because the lady in question has a dark secret. She is Stephen of Blois' bastard daughter, and the countess disapproves of her. She was absent from court when we returned from where we had been fighting on the shores of the Black Sea, and it was then that Thomas became anxious to return to England. Perhaps she is here already.'

'In London?'

'Perhaps. Until shortly before we left, our conversation was all to do with our return to Walsingham. By the time we were taking ship, Thomas was intent on delaying his return in order to conduct some sort of secret business in London.'

'You know that we have a new king?' his mother enquired as she steered him though the manor house door and called for wine.

114

'We heard while we were still in Blois, where we were sent by Count Robert when we first arrived in Normandy. We fought under the command of his brother-in-law Count Stephen.'

'Then you would not have learned that Wilfrid here was imprisoned by the former king for almost two years?'

'No, but it would not surprise me. If I have learned anything, it is that kings and counts are not to be trusted.'

'You heard what Geoffrey said about the treachery in the courts of Europe,' Joan reminded Wilfrid over supper. 'You have enough experience of your own to know that, yet you plan to return to King Henry so soon?'

Geoffrey nodded sagely across the table, where they all sat enjoying a celebratory meal.

'I gave my pledge,' Wilfrid replied stubbornly, 'and I have already agreed that you may come with me. We also have another reason to journey to London now — we must find out what has delayed Thomas.'

'You *did* promise that I could come with you,' Matilda reminded him.

He smiled as he reached out and nuzzled her cheek. 'Indeed I did, and indeed you shall. We leave whenever we can make the necessary arrangements with those we will leave behind to manage the estate. Let us see what King Henry deems to be so important for the security of his crown.'

XVI

'You kept your promise,' King Henry beamed as Wilfrid was ushered into the presence. 'This speaks much for your integrity, and therefore for the mission that I have for you. Your chamber is to your liking?'

'Indeed, sire,' Wilfrid replied politely, omitting to mention Joan's expression of disgust at the layer of dust above one of the wall hangings, 'and I have taken the liberty of bringing my wife and daughter with me on this occasion. My daughter has never been to court, and it has been some time since my wife was at Westminster, in the days when she served the last Saxon king, Harold.'

'Served him in what way?'

'With food and drink, sire,' Wilfrid replied with a slightly embarrassed smile.

Henry laughed. 'You must present her at some stage during your stay here, which hopefully will not be long, since I require you to take to the road on my behalf without any further delay.'

'For what reason, sire?'

'In a moment. Reference to your wife's improved status reminds me that during our last audience, I omitted to advise you that I have confirmed you in your estates. You remain "Sir Wilfrid Walsingham".'

'Thank you, sire. I had not thought to enquire.'

'Another good sign that I am served by a man whose ambition will not prove to be either his downfall or mine. I wish to restore England to what it was in my father's time — a land in which loyalty is rewarded, men are advanced for the right reasons, and false flatterers are denied access to court. You of course remember Ranulf Flambard?'

'Indeed I do, sire, and the last I saw of him he was a sycophant to your brother William.'

Henry sighed. 'Flambard and other evildoers grew rich at the nation's expense while he was Treasurer. I hope he retains memories of happier days, because now he is languishing downriver in the new Tower that his patron built — rather fitting, I thought. There is now a new Treasurer, Herbert of Winchester, and he has pledged to serve me honestly. This will be the flavour of the monarchy that I shall conduct. Read this.'

He handed Wilfrid a long parchment, the ink on which was still black and legible, suggesting that it had been created recently. It was headed 'Charter of Liberties', and after the preliminary greetings it contained pledges by Henry regarding how he intended to govern the country, and assurances that there would be no abuses of power. First and foremost, it gave an assurance that clerical benefices and succession to estates would not be held to ransom by the Crown, nor would there be any taxation levied on clergymen succeeding to office, sons succeeding to estates, or widows seeking to remarry. In addition, all unjust debts formerly due to King William Rufus were cancelled. There was more of a similar nature, but Henry was clearly anxious for Wilfrid's initial response.

'This should gladden many a heart, sire, and put paid to any fear that your reign will be as despotic, or as grasping, as your brother's,' Wilfrid assured him.

Henry frowned. 'You would think so, naturally. But it has not proved so. Archbishop Anselm regards me as the anti-Christ, the earls and barons are muttering that my brother Robert would be better for England, and as usual Saxons such as yourself consider themselves shackled to a Norman usurper.'

'Not this Saxon, sire.'

Henry smiled. 'You *were* one of those who stood against my father in the Saxon cause, were you not?'

'Indeed I was, but I was fighting for my country, and the life we knew. I then went on to serve as an interpreter to your father, seeking to prevent unnecessary bloodshed due to a failure of language, and since then I have had cause to learn that England is far better ruled by one king overall than a group of petty barons, each with their own fiefdom, and forever fighting among themselves.'

'Like my brothers and I, you mean?' Henry raised his hand. 'No, do not seek to deny that we sons of Duke William have made a complete mess of ruling England and Normandy. But once I can get the barons on my side, it will be different. And that is why I require your services.'

'I doubt that a mere Saxon such as myself could sway a Norman baron,' Wilfrid objected.

Henry nodded. 'Indeed you could not, simply by being yourself. But it is what I wish you to discover that will ease my smooth passage to English sovereignty.'

'Sire?'

'Let us sit and enjoy some wine while I tell you a sad tale. What do you know of Rufus's death?'

'Merely that he died during a hunting accident.'

'And were you told that I was present?'

'No, sire.'

'That's something, at least,' Henry muttered as he signalled to an usher to bring wine, then pour two goblets, one of which he handed to Wilfrid. 'It was in the New Forest, where we were hunting, late in the day. There was a strong sunset, and it half blinded us as we sought out a suitable stag, armed with our bows. There was a stray shot, and Rufus was fatally pierced through the chest.'

'You are sure it was a stray shot?' Wilfrid enquired. 'Forgive me, but there has been much muttering regarding the forest laws, and the royal forests are populated by many men who are skilled with the bow, some of whom might have meant your brother harm.'

'Already you prove the wisdom of my choice, but let me set your mind at rest on that point. There were five of us in all, including Rufus, and the shot must have come from one of us.'

'But not you?'

Henry grimaced. 'You have identified your mission. I wish you to prove that it was not me.'

'There are those who claim that it was?'

'There are *many* who claim that it was, and no doubt countless more prepared to believe it, but who remain silent. It suits my brother Robert to maintain that false accusation, since it will give the semblance of justification for the invasion he is known to be planning in order to challenge my right to rule England. Then there are the former "friends" of Rufus, who have every reason to fear the justice that is heading their way. Finally, those of my subjects who have no predisposition to suspect me, but who may be swayed by others.'

'But what grounds could they have for such a vile slander?'

Henry looked shamefaced as he took another sip of wine. 'I was persuaded — perhaps wrongly — by my other companions in the hunt to lose no time in racing to Winchester, where the royal Treasury is still housed. I ordered that it be locked down and securely guarded, on the royal command, and I did so for the sake of England, as you must believe if you are to be of best service to me. The last thing I wanted was another squabble for the throne, during which the only ones to suffer would have been the honest, simple folk of England. From Winchester I rode hard to London, whose bishop was bullied — by me, I regret to say — into crowning me King of England before the news of Rufus's death had reached the rest of the nation. Archbishop Anselm was still in his self-imposed exile, and even now he refuses to return.'

Wilfrid thought long and hard, sipping on his wine. 'You must advise me of the identities of the others who were present when Rufus died, and how each of them was positioned at the fatal moment.'

Henry looked into the middle distance as his memory replayed the scene. 'There were of course many in the main party, largely foresters, grooms and suchlike. But only five of us moved forward through the undergrowth. If you know the New Forest, you will appreciate that it is largely composed of oaks, beech and ash, with thick clumps of bracken and gorse that hinder progress, and make a considerable amount of noise as huntsmen move through it. Enough to startle the quarry, at least. For that reason, we hunters tend to follow the paths through the foliage that have been beaten by others before us, and so it was that day. We split into two groups.'

'The names, sire?' Wilfrid prompted him.

Henry nodded as he continued to stare blankly ahead of him. 'The group that took the left path consisted of myself, and the two brothers Gilbert and Roger Clare. We were slightly ahead of the second party that took the right track, where the going was easier. That second group consisted of Rufus and Walter Tyrrell, one of the best huntsmen in England at that time.'

'And then?'

'We heard the sound of a deer being startled from its hiding place. It was slightly to the right of my group, and slightly behind. I think we were the ones who disturbed it. Anyway, it flew off to our right, and must have been right in the line of sight of Rufus and Walter, but as I already mentioned, the setting sun shone brightly in all our eyes.'

'And it was then that Rufus was fatally injured?'

Henry closed his eyes with a slight shudder, then continued. 'Indeed. I believe that Rufus loosed an arrow that wounded the beast, before running into the clearing just behind us, and to our right. He was followed, I believe, by Walter Tyrrell, and then, as we moved right to close in on what must have been a wounded beast, we heard Rufus give a scream of pain. We blundered through the bracken towards him, and found him face-down, with an arrow piercing his chest. Walter turned him over with his boot, and it was clear that Rufus could not long survive. It was Gilbert who reached down and confirmed that he was already dead, then he accused Walter Tyrrell of the death.'

'And Tyrrell's response?'

'He denied it, and claimed that the fatal arrow had come from his left. But then Gilbert Clare found the shaft of the arrow that had killed Rufus, where it had fallen after he'd tried to pull it from his chest. It was one of a set of arrows made specially for my brother by the Royal Fletcher, Giles Montferrat. They had been presented to Rufus that morning — a set of six with golden flights. But before we set out, Rufus handed two of them to Walter Tyrrell, saying it was only appropriate that the better marksman should have the best arrows. When we examined Walter's quiver, he had only one of them left. He tried to explain that he had fired the first at a wild boar, but when no-one believed him he turned and ran.'

'But you now believe him?'

'Yes. At the time his sudden flight seemed suspicious, and I was too preoccupied with claiming the throne. But since then I have given the matter much thought. Walter was one of the finest bowmen in England, and the fatal arrow must have come from somewhere ahead of Rufus, whereas Walter was behind him as my brother broke cover and moved into the clearing. I believe that Walter may not have been the guilty one, but he was hesitant to say so publicly because of the greater suspicion that would then fall upon me.'

Wilfrid thought for a moment, fixing in his mind the scene that had just been described to him, then he looked directly into Henry's eyes. 'If we discount Tyrrell, then the fatal arrow must have come from one of the three of you who were to Rufus's left. If it was not you, then it must have been either Gilbert or Roger Clare, and each of them must be aware of that fact. Where are they now?'

'In Suffolk and Kent. You remember Richard Fitz Gilbert?'

'The man who was left in charge of England when your father returned to Normandy two years after his victory at Pevensey? The man who rebelled against him later, and was imprisoned instead of being done to death?'

'The very same. Gilbert and Roger are his sons, and they became favourites of my brother Rufus because of their willingness to join him in order to fight the Scots. While their father was consigned to a monastery, where he recently died, his sons were allowed to retain their lands, and Gilbert is currently in Tonbridge, in Kent. He has rebuilt the castle, and lives in considerable splendour. His younger brother Roger is now the Earl of Hertford. You should also know that Walter Tyrrell is married to Adeliza Fitz Gilbert, and is therefore brother-in-law to both Gilbert and Roger.'

'Where is Tyrrell now?'

'He had estates near Rouen, to which he fled within hours of Rufus's death. Rouen, as you probably know, is in Normandy, and I fear that Tyrrell has been granted sanctuary by my brother Robert, who contests my claim to the English throne. I also believe that it is Tyrrell who has supplied Robert with the excuse to invade England, as he is planning to do in the near future. That excuse, of course, is the accusation that I killed Rufus in order to acquire the crown, which is why it is so important that you find the truth of the matter.'

'You have allowed the Clare brothers to retain their estates, even though one of them may have killed your brother?'

'Yes, to my shame,' Henry replied as he stared into his wine goblet. 'They are powerful nobles, and they command a large following of friends and sympathisers. I cannot afford to lose their support at this time, given the faction that is against me even here in England.'

'And who leads this enemy faction?'

'You will not be surprised, I think, to learn that chief among them is your old enemy Roger Bigod. His vast estates in Norfolk and Suffolk bring him great wealth, and as sheriff of both counties he is in a strong position to influence others to enlist under his banner. He is known to be loyal to Robert, and although he has assured me of his fealty, and was one of the witnesses to the Charter of Liberties upon my coronation, it is my strong belief that he will rise up in support of Robert, should he invade. Then there is William of Breteuil, who spoke out against my coronation, on the grounds that the barons should be entitled to choose between myself and Robert. It was fortunate that Robert was then on crusade, and the majority of the barons preferred the certainty of my rule rather than the irresponsibility of a ruler who had pledged Normandy for ten thousand marks in order to finance a crusading army that has recently returned with little to show for the many lives they squandered.'

'One of which might have been that of my son Thomas, although I hear that he may be back here in London, not that he has been in touch with the family,' Wilfrid observed ruefully.

'You have not heard? Your son is indeed back in London, and here at court, as an emissary of Count Stephen of Blois, who wants nothing to do with Robert's evil scheme to depose me. He seeks to sign a peace treaty that will ensure his neutrality, and he has offered to guard my lands in the Cotentin, which adjoin his. There will probably be a marriage to further the peace, and since he is married to my sister, any offspring will of course be first cousins to any children I may have.'

'You have not yet married?'

'Why should I, when the court seems well supplied with beautiful women? But I am advised that I must, and it is suggested that I might look to Scotland for a bride, thereby securing our northern border.'

'This man who has come from Blois with the peace offering — how can you be sure he is my son?' Wilfrid enquired, both puzzled and hurt that Thomas could have delayed returning to Walsingham, or at least sending word through Geoffrey de Faverches, who apparently remained ignorant of Thomas's real reason for his return to London.

'I assume that Sir Thomas Walsingham *is* your son?' Henry enquired. 'He certainly resembles you. Although, of course, he's much younger.'

'Twenty years younger,' Wilfrid admitted, 'but I had no idea he had been knighted, presumably by his new overlord of Blois. His companion on the Crusade, Geoffrey de Faverches, made no mention that Thomas had been knighted, but his reason for that may simply have been jealousy. But where is *Sir* Thomas now?'

'He is probably still here at court, although he will shortly be returning to Blois with my response to the proposed peace treaty. I should perhaps delay you no longer, so you may seek him out and welcome him back to England.'

'More likely cuff his ear, for his failure to contact his parents on his return.'

'It is of some comfort to me to learn that the disrespect of sons for fathers was not confined to the House of Normandy. But lose no time in finding the truth of Rufus's death. Where will you begin?'

'Which of the Clare brothers do you most suspect?' Wilfrid asked.

'Gilbert, without doubt. He is the older brother, and is a more skilled archer. He also seemed to bear some ill-will towards Tyrrell, although I know not what was the cause of that.'

'Then I shall begin in Kent,' Wilfrid advised Henry as he rose to his feet. 'I will of course keep you well informed, but it may be that I will be met with resistance, and a refusal to answer questions.'

Henry reached out to the table on which he had replaced the copy of the Charter of Liberties, and slid another single vellum sheet from under it, handing it up to Wilfrid. 'There is my commission. Anyone who defies you will be imprisoned for treason.'

'Just like old times,' Wilfrid smiled ironically as he bowed and left the royal presence.

XVII

Matilda was fascinated by every new sight, sound and activity at court. She had spent almost all her life at Walsingham, and most of her adult years working in her aunt's orphanage and school attached to the convent. Several times she had considered taking holy orders like Aunt Elva — or 'Sister Grace' — and when her cousin Elston had entered the monastery at Ely, she had almost taken the veil herself. But something deep inside her craved a family of her own, despite the absence of any suitable husband within the narrow confines of a country estate in Norfolk. Now she had come across a different world.

The women wore brightly coloured clothing, and everywhere they floated down the corridors of the Palace of Westminster they were followed by a waft of rich perfumes. Their hair was immaculately groomed, and they were always attended by servant girls who were described as 'ladies'. The men at court were tall, handsome, gallant and confident to the point of rudeness. Matilda was aware that she was not lacking in beauty, but it was the sort of beauty generated by fresh air and healthy exercise; she was simply dressed in her best gown of autumn hue, and her fair hair swung freely down to her shoulders, without any ornate headgear. Her eyes were cornflower blue, and her figure was ample but modestly restrained.

However, she did not lack lascivious glances from finely dressed nobles and burly men at arms as she wandered freely around the palace hallways, yards and outbuildings, taking it all in. She'd had no idea that this world existed three days ago, and she hoped that her parents would not decide to return to

Walsingham until she had seen everything she wished to see, and filled her mind with memories she could carry back to her more humdrum existence.

She was heading towards the stables, hoping once again to catch the eye of some handsome man at arms who might perhaps engage her in conversation, when she heard her name being called in a hoarse whisper. She turned, and from behind an empty wagon peered the face of the brother she had not seen for two years, his fingers to his lips in a request for silence. He slid slowly into view, dressed in full chainmail, and with a huge sword hanging from his belt.

'Thomas!' she whispered with delight, and rushed forward to embrace him. As she did so, he pulled her further behind the wagon and looked apprehensively towards the palace buildings from which she had recently walked.

'Our parents must not know I am here! And what, for that matter, are all of you doing here? I could hardly believe my eyes when I saw the three of you dismounting in the stable yard.'

'You saw us arrive?'

'My horse was being re-shod after its long journey from Blois.'

'Where's that?'

'Over in France. I brought a message for King Henry from my former master Count Stephen of Blois.'

'What was in it? And why do you no longer serve him?'

'Too many questions, without answering mine. What brings you here?'

'The king has some duty or other for Father to discharge, in exchange for his release.'

'Release from where?'

'You didn't know he had been imprisoned by the former King William? He almost died.'

'I have been halfway round the world during the past two years. I fought in a Crusade, and I fought for Count Stephen in Blois. Did my former companion Geoffrey not tell you any of this?'

'Only that you were safe, and here in London. Do you plan to return to Blois without seeing our parents?'

'I had not intended to — at least, not immediately, although I have important unfinished business there. But the document I gave to King Henry seemed to greatly interest him, and he has instructed me to return to Blois at once with his response. It is in my saddlebag, over in the stables there, and I was just preparing to ride out when I saw you wandering across the stable yard as if you were back home in the daffodil field. Do you not fear any harm from these rough soldiers?'

'What possible harm could they threaten, when they are noble and loyal soldiers of the king who our father serves?'

Thomas shook his head in disbelief. 'Easy to see that you were raised and educated in a convent. I take it from the absence of severe clothing that you haven't yet joined Aunt Elva in a life of poverty, chastity and obedience?'

'No, and *definitely* not, after witnessing all this grandeur, and learning that there is another life beyond Walsingham. It must be *so* exciting for you, living in this world.'

'It has its darker side,' Thomas replied enigmatically. 'But when do you intend to return to Walsingham? You *will* return, I hope?'

'I suppose so,' Matilda replied with a pout. 'But not soon, I hope.'

'Is the orphanage still there?'

'Of course, why?'

'And do you still assist in its day to day care?'

'Yes, but again — why do you want to know?'

'Is there room for one more child?'

'We take any child in need, you must remember that. But why are you enquiring?'

'Would you take a French child?'

'Every child comes from God, regardless of where it is born. Stop being so evasive. Have you adopted an orphan?'

'In a manner of speaking,' Thomas grinned. 'It is the child of a daughter of the Count of Blois, and she wishes it to be spirited away from the court over there.'

'Why?'

'Because it is illegitimate.'

'So was our former King William, the one who conquered England. There is no disgrace in that these days, as you should know, being a man of the world.'

'This one is special.'

'In what way "special"?'

Thomas hesitated for a moment, then decided that Matilda was entitled to the truth, in view of what he was asking of her. 'It's mine.'

'I thought you said it was the child of a royal princess of Blois.'

'Not quite. I said that it was the child of a daughter of the Count of Blois. A daughter who is herself illegitimate, and has been ill used by the countess since the day of her birth. She does not wish for the same to happen to our daughter.'

'So it's a girl? And she's yours? So you've been … you know? With that count's daughter?'

'Many times, and one day I hope to marry her. But in the immediate future, the child must be brought up safely, but in obscurity, and I can't think of anywhere that fits both of those requirements better than your orphanage in Walsingham.'

'And what do you propose that I tell our parents? I can hardly claim that it's mine.'

'You most certainly cannot,' Thomas agreed. 'Apart from having to admit to doing things that are against your beliefs, and possibly contrary to your nature, the mother of the child is as dark in hair and general colouring as you are fair, and the child appears to take after her in appearance.'

'What do *you* know of my nature?' Matilda demanded with a blush. 'I certainly could not bring myself to do carnal things with those pimply boys in Walsingham, but since casting my eyes on these more, well, more *muscled* — soldiers, I'm only glad that I didn't turn my back on things like that. Do you have any companions who're seeking a clean country girl for a bride with whom to settle down to a farming life?'

Thomas burst out laughing. 'If only you knew! But please, dearest sister, do not be misled and betrayed by any of these oafs you see around the palace. They would strip you, first of your clothing, and then of your honour. They would probably do you some considerable damage, were you to lie with one of them.'

Matilda went bright red and punched her brother on the chest, only to cry out when her knuckles were grazed by the rough chainmail. '*Now* look what you've made me do!'

'That's nothing compared with what any of these men that you seem to admire would do to you, so be well warned. And you agree to take my child?'

'At the orphanage we take *any* child. But how will you manage to bring her all the way to Walsingham?'

Thomas was floored by that question, to which he had given no thought. 'I have no skill in handling small babies, so it may be that you'll have to send someone from the orphanage down here to London. Or, since you seem so taken by it, you may wish to come down yourself, when I send you word. I have to leave now — go back to our parents, and say nothing of having seen me, or of our conversation.'

'Do you not wish to see them again?'

'Yes, but I don't want to have to answer all these questions. So, give me your farewell, try not to cut yourself on my armour, and keep safe from all these ruffians.'

When Matilda returned to her parents, Joan immediately noticed her grazed knuckles and proceeded to clean them with a wet rag. 'How did you come to cut your hand in the first place?' she asked.

'I caught it on the rough stonework of a wall as I was wandering in from the yard,' Matilda lied glibly. She asked God for His forgiveness as her father examined the damage more carefully.

'It will soon heal, in my experience. It's the sort of graze you get when you catch your hand on a suit of chainmail. I hope you haven't been getting too familiar with a soldier, Tilly.'

'Of course not,' Matilda insisted, 'although it would not be for lack of invitation. If we are to abide here for much longer, I might well find myself a suitable husband among them.'

'All the better that we'll be leaving tomorrow, then,' Wilfrid observed as Joan winced at the mere thought.

'Are we going home so soon?' Matilda pouted.

'No, we are heading south of the river, to Kent,' her father replied. 'Perhaps you'll meet with the man of your dreams there.'

'And perhaps not, if I have my way,' Joan replied tersely.

XVIII

Thomas guided his horse down the wooded hill and across the bridge over the Loire, gazing up at the heavily fortified palace walls and cursing the weakness that had led to his return. When he had left, a few months earlier, he had convinced himself that the final look back at the crenulated walls of the ancient chateau would be his last; that somehow or other Lady Emma would find a way of joining him in England along with their child. It had never occurred to him, when grasping the justification for his return to England when Count Stephen had asked him to convey a document to King Henry, that there would be a reply. He had made a feeble effort to refuse the return journey, but his new English monarch had not been in the mood for Thomas's false modesty, or protestations of unworthiness, and had taken Thomas at face value as an emissary of Blois.

During the two weeks or so it had taken Thomas to journey back, he had decided that if it worked in one direction, it might work in the other. If King Henry had mistaken him for an authorised emissary of Blois, instead of the mere carrier of a message, why should Stephen of Blois not treat Thomas as representing the far more powerful King of England? If nothing else, it would ensure that he was not refused access to the palace, and it might even raise his standing at the Court of Blois to the level at which he might be seriously considered as a suitable marriage partner for the illegitimate daughter of the count. It was worth a try, if he could keep his nerve for long enough. But even if he finished up outside the chateau walls, he might have the opportunity to see Emma, and perhaps even their daughter.

Emma had said, in her message through the mouth of her servant, that she would find some way of crossing the Channel to England to be with him. That might have been why she wanted Thomas to take the child first, to make her journey that much easier. If so, then perhaps he had acted rashly in seeking to have their daughter hidden away in an obscure orphanage in deepest Norfolk, since a lady as grand as Emma, notwithstanding her illegitimacy, would expect to be received at the English Court, and not offered a basic, if comfortable, existence in the grounds of a holy shrine and convent.

Thomas took a deep breath and maintained an air of affected arrogance, as he announced to the Captain of the Palace Guard that he came as an emissary of King Henry of England, and had urgent and secret business with the count. The battle-scarred old warrior looked pointedly behind Thomas's mount.

'From a king, are yer? Where's yer escort, then?'

'Did I not say that the matter was secret?' Thomas replied down his nose as he raised himself higher in the saddle. 'How secret would my arrival be if announced with a fanfare of trumpets, and accompanied by a hundred liveried men at arms?'

'I know yer face, don't I? Ain't you that English one what 'ung around the count fer a while back there, an' got the Lady Emma with child?'

'I don't need to explain myself to you, you impudent oaf!' Thomas replied with one nervous eye on the massive sword hanging from the man's belt. 'Just earn your pittance and tell the count that Sir Thomas Walsingham is here with a dispatch from King Henry of England.'

Ten minutes later, Count Stephen looked down at him from his high backed, padded chair in the style of a throne with a suspicious frown. 'I hope that this is not some extravagant ruse designed to enable you to see my daughter again. If so, you are in for a disappointment, as well as a few weeks in my dungeons.'

Thomas put on an air of affront. 'I'm sure that King Henry would not be pleased to learn that his emissary was treated with such discourtesy.'

'According to the Captain of my Guard, you have some sort of message for me from your master.'

'A little more than that, my lord. It is, or so I am advised, his formal response to your offer to enter into a treaty with him. I know no more than that, obviously. In view of the secrecy urged upon me by his Majesty as he entrusted me with this despatch, I was not even prepared to disclose that much information to the man who halted my progress into your palace. He behaved little better than a tavern brawler who'd acquired a suit of chainmail.'

Stephen smiled faintly at the apt description, and held out his hand for the document. Thomas extracted it from the pouch inside his jacket, where it had lain since he had first been handed it in Westminster Palace. He remained standing patiently while Stephen began to read it. Halfway through the process, his smile grew broader, and he beckoned for Thomas to take a seat.

Eventually, Stephen looked up and asked, 'Who exactly *is* this Herbert of Winchester?'

'I have no idea, my lord.'

'He is described here as the Royal Treasurer, yet you have no further knowledge of him? How familiar *are* you with the inner workings of the English Court, exactly?'

Thomas thought quickly. 'Of late, matters there have been, shall we say, somewhat confused, my lord. Those who previously occupied high office have been consigned to the dungeons, and replaced with low-born men the king can trust. Men such as myself and my father.'

'Your father being?'

'Sir Wilfrid de Walsingham, who is rumoured to have been recruited by Henry for a special mission, the precise nature of which even I am not aware. I would not even have known of that, had my sister not advised me when we met at Westminster Palace, where she was choosing a husband for herself.'

'How senior is the office of Royal Treasurer?'

'Very senior, my lord. It is reserved for only the most trusted confidants, and those closest to the throne. May I enquire why you wish to know?'

'No, you may not. How long were you thinking of remaining with us?'

Thomas took the warning from the tone of his voice. 'I have completed my mission, my lord. Unless you require me to remain while you compose a further reply to my master in England, then there is nothing further to detain me.'

'Indeed there is not, at present. If it satisfies your curiosity, you should know that the Lady Emma has been banished from court by the countess, and is currently in Bayonne, surrounded by her women. They, I am told, take it in turns to look after your child, along with some physician or other, since she is reported to have tired of it already. She has been named "Elinor", should you be interested.'

'How could a man not be interested in the welfare of his own child?' Thomas replied warmly. 'And should it indeed be the case that she no longer has any interest in it, there is somewhere in England where I could arrange for it to be given a fine life among God-fearing women.'

'A nunnery, you mean?' Stephen enquired frostily. 'You propose to lose my granddaughter in a nunnery?'

'She would not be lost, my lord,' Thomas hastened to explain. 'The convent in question is on my family's estate, and my own sister is in charge of an orphanage there that…'

'Enough!' Stephen bellowed. 'No granddaughter of the Count of Blois will ever be accounted an orphan. It was bad enough that my daughter was never recognised here at court, and what you are suggesting is totally unacceptable to me. However, it may be that there will come a need for you to take the child into your care in England, if either of these latest proposals from King Henry comes to fruition.'

'And what are they, my lord?'

'None of your damned business — yet. But you might wish to persuade your King Henry to commission you to escort through England a delegation that will shortly travel from here, whichever of Henry's proposals I decide to adopt. If neither, then there will be no such delegation. You will be accommodated here for as many days as you require in order to rest both yourself and your horse.'

'Indeed, my lord,' Thomas mumbled politely as he bowed and left the count's presence.

Why was Count Stephen suddenly so hostile to the man who had once saved his life, and had ridden faithfully by his side on crusade? Was the tide going out between Blois and England, or was Stephen anxious not to be seen to be too friendly with one brother-in-law now that the other — the one closest to his own borders — was back in Normandy, and furious about Henry's seizure of the English crown?

XIX

Wilfrid, Joan and Matilda heaved a sigh of relief as they breasted the hill side by side on their tired horses. They saw that the outer bailey of the partly reconstructed castle was well to the north of the flood plain of the River Medway that they had been warned about at the abbey they had left that morning, on the third day of their journey south from London.

Tonbridge was the family seat of Gilbert de Clare, the first on the list of those whom Wilfrid needed to question regarding the death of the late King William Rufus. He hoped that the commission that was tucked into his tunic would be sufficient to get them past the gatehouse. Matilda gazed, awestruck, at the height that the stonemasons had reached on their flimsy platform thirty feet above the ground. They were mortaring another course of heavy stones into place as they reached the platform on the pulley at which sweat-drenched men were heaving. The new arrivals trotted under the face of the wall and announced their business to the Captain of the Guard, who was summoned by the minion on gate duty.

While they waited for the soldier who could barely read and write to struggle through the commission vellum that was written in French, Wilfrid reminded himself of the somewhat chequered career of the man he would be closely questioning if they ever got past the gate. Gilbert de Clare, along with his brother Roger, had staged a rebellion against William Rufus twelve years before the monarch's untimely death, and the original castle that had occupied this site, in which the brothers had dug in for a siege, had been all but demolished when the royal forces prevailed. Then, curiously, both brothers had been not only pardoned, but also raised to favour at Rufus's court, to the point at which they had been part of his hunting party on the fatal day. They had also been granted leave to rebuild their castle, and the noisy, dusty work being conducted above Wilfrid and his family was the final stage in this reconstruction.

Why had Rufus been so forgiving, when in so many other instances — such as Wilfrid's — he had been so ruthless and cruel? Why had he given the brothers not only a second chance, but also the close access to him that came with being one of his inner circle at court? Did they have some hold over him, and if so, what had it been? Were they perhaps saved by the intervention of someone close to Rufus? Flambard, perhaps? Had Rufus been nursing, close to his bosom, a viper that would one day be his undoing?

The heavy gate to the outer keep creaked open, and there in the opening stood a man dressed in the livery of red chevrons on a field of yellow. Wilfrid recalled him from his days in the service of the Fitz Gilbert father. The man identified himself as the steward, and addressed Wilfrid in deferential tones.

'My master has instructed that a suite of rooms be placed at your disposal in the south wing, which is the one overlooking the river, where the breezes are stronger. I have ordered that food and wine be brought to you without delay, and when my master has partaken of dinner, he will be pleased to speak with you, and learn of your business.'

'He made a point of not inviting us to dine with him,' Joan huffed as she made her customary inspection of the fabrics in the room. She frowned as she gazed towards the river. 'There certainly *are* river breezes at this casement — more like a howling bloody gale, if you ask me.'

'May I go for a walk after we have eaten?' Matilda enquired eagerly.

Wilfrid nodded, then lowered his voice. 'You may, but keep your hands off any chainmail this time. Your mother won't believe excuses about brick walls *every* time.'

Matilda suppressed the urge to advise Wilfrid whose chainmail she had grazed her knuckles on, concluding that this was not the time, and not wishing to say anything that might lead to the withdrawal of parental permission to explore another new and exciting place.

The midday meal of fish, freshly baked bread, roast pork, fruits, nuts and cheese was brought in by a small team of servers, who laid it all out on the trestle they had just erected, and two serving girls followed close behind with wine and small beer. Since their only meal that day had been weak porridge in a seemingly impoverished monastery, they tucked into the food with relish. An hour later, Wilfrid requested, and was granted, an audience with Gilbert de Clare, a tall bluff warrior with a red beard that was in urgent need of a trim.

Gilbert examined the commission that the king had given Wilfrid, then looked up with a smile that appeared to be a little forced. 'Henry does not reveal the precise nature of your commission, but it is obviously so important to him that he has deemed a refusal to co-operate to be treason. So what do you need to know?'

Wilfrid made a mental note of the familiarity with which Gilbert had mentioned the king, almost as if they were brothers. Here was a man who must be approached with the utmost tact, he concluded as he kept the introduction as broad as he could. 'You were present when the late King William met his unfortunate death, I am advised.'

'I was indeed. A most distressing business.'

'I am requested by his Majesty to acquaint myself as fully as possible with the facts. What do you recall of the matter, if anything?'

'I recall a great deal,' Gilbert insisted, 'since an event so tragic does not occur in one's presence more than once in a lifetime, it is to be hoped.'

'So what do you recall?'

Gilbert closed his eyes. 'There were five of us. Myself, my brother Roger, King Henry as he became, Rufus the King — and Walter Tyrrell, the man whose arrow proved to be the fatal one.'

'What reason have you for the conclusion that it was Tyrrell who loosed the fatal shot?'

'It was his arrow.'

'And how could one arrow be distinguished from another?'

Gilbert smiled. 'You are clearly no archer. Every arrow is fitted with a "flight", or a "fletching" as it is called — a cluster of feathers arranged in such a way as to give what would otherwise be a mere length of wood its ability to pass through the air towards its target.'

'Forgive me, but I *do* have some basic knowledge of archery,' Wilfrid replied with heavy sarcasm.

'My apologies. But you must therefore know that no two fletchings are the same, any more than the wood from which the shaft is constructed, or the method used to sharpen or reinforce the point that delivers the wound. By these means, a skilled fletcher can identify each arrow, and distinguish one from another.'

'What is the significance of this?' Wilfrid enquired.

'When Rufus was shot, it was in the chest, and before he fell into the leaf litter, he attempted to pull the arrow out. Instead, it snapped, and the fletching fell into the undergrowth, from where I retrieved it.'

'And it was possible to identify whose it was?'

'Indeed, only too easily. As we were dining that day, ahead of setting out to hunt, the king's own fletcher brought him a new set of arrows, specially made for Rufus. According to the fletcher, they were very special.'

'The fletcher's name was Giles Montferrat?' Wilfrid asked.

Gilbert's expression became wary. 'You are obviously well informed, so I'm not sure of the need for you to question me, but yes, that was the man. Still is, I believe.'

'Montferrat is still in the king's service?'

'Why would he not be? No blame can be attached to him for Rufus's death. He may be found in the royal armoury at Westminster. Do you wish me to continue?'

'Yes, sorry — please do.'

'Well, these special arrows had a very distinctive fletching of gold, and Montferrat assured Rufus that he had reinforced their tips with a special metal, so as to penetrate the strongest deer's hide. He gave Rufus the entire set of six, then Rufus made a great show of presenting Walter Tyrrell with two of them, flattering him by saying that since he was the best marksman of us all, it was only fitting that he should have some of the best arrows.'

'And it was one of these that killed the king?'

'Indeed. When I made a search of the ground near where Rufus had fallen, I found the broken shaft of one of these special arrows, with the gold fletching. Rufus had attempted to pull the arrow from his chest, but it had snapped. In the belief that it could not have come from Rufus's quiver, I pointed out the obvious fact that the fatal arrow must have been one of the two supplied to Tyrrell. This appeared to be confirmed by the fact that when we examined his quiver, there was only one of the original two arrows left.'

'And how did he respond to this accusation?'

'He tried to deny it, with some story about having fired one at a boar earlier that afternoon, but none of us could remember that. Walter looked more and more guilty the longer we continued to accuse him. Then he turned and ran.'

'If we assume for the moment that it was indeed his arrow, could it not have been an unlucky accident?' Wilfrid enquired. 'Such things have been known.'

Gilbert gave a light, dismissive laugh. 'Walter Tyrrell was at that time one of the finest bowmen in England. Such a man could not possibly have loosed a shot in error.'

'And indeed,' Wilfrid remarked casually, 'he must have taken deliberate aim, and succeeded in making his arrow project in a half-circle.'

Gilbert's face set like a mask. 'What is your meaning?'

'Was Tyrrell not behind Rufus when the fatal arrow was loosed?'

'He may have been — he may not have been. We were not in a position to judge.'

'So where *was* everyone positioned, exactly?'

'Rufus and Tyrrell were in one group, off to the right, and my brother and I, along with Henry, formed a second group to the left, and slightly behind the first group.'

'And where were each of you positioned, in the group on the left?'

'Henry was in the lead, as I recall, only a few feet ahead of me. It was difficult to know precisely who was where, because it was late afternoon and the sunset was particularly strong. We either had to look down at the ground, or — if we looked up — we had to shield our eyes. I cannot be sure that it was

Henry ahead of me, since I only saw the heels of the boots ahead as I looked down at the ground, to avoid being blinded. It could have been my brother Roger.'

'Assuming that it was Henry ahead of you, where would Roger have been?'

'Slightly behind me, and to my right — closer to where Rufus and Tyrrell were walking on the track to the right, although as I recall the paths were beginning to diverge. And they were slightly ahead of us on the right-hand track.'

'So what was the first you knew that there had been an "accident", shall we say?'

'We heard a scream of some sort from Rufus, just after we'd startled a deer — or at least, I assume it was a deer — off to our right. It would have been directly in the line of sight of Rufus and Walter. For a brief second, I thought that what I'd heard was a shout of triumph, telling us that Rufus had found his mark. But there was also fear in the sound, and we all rushed off to our right. Tyrrell stood there with his mouth open in what was almost certainly feigned shock, and Rufus lay down on the ground. I turned him over with my boot, and checked the heartbeat at that point in the neck where it's possible to feel the blood coursing, but there was nothing, and I told the others that the king was dead.'

'What did you see as you first ran over?' Wilfrid enquired as disingenuously as he could.

'As I just said, the king lying in the leaf litter.'

'Then how did you know that he had tried to pull the arrow from his chest?'

Gilbert appeared to falter for a moment, and his smile looked even more frozen as the reply came to him. 'Walter Tyrrell must have told me. I didn't actually see that happen.'

'But from what you told me earlier, it was all a scene of shocked confusion when you arrived at the body, and the only conversation that took place concerned Tyrrell's seeming responsibility for the death.'

'As I *also* mentioned earlier,' Gilbert insisted, 'it was a very tense atmosphere, full of emotion. It's not every day you see your king lying dead at your feet.'

'So you took Tyrrell's sudden flight as a token of his guilt?'

'Who would not?'

'Did you not try to prevent his escape? After all, it appeared that he had just killed Rufus. Did you not demand that he remain, or seek to detain him?'

'It all happened so quickly, and there was no conversation regarding what was to happen next.'

'But there was, was there not?' Wilfrid corrected him. 'According to King Henry, someone urged him to ride hard to Winchester and seize command of the Treasury. Was that person you?'

'I don't recall anything of that sort being said,' Gilbert insisted. 'It really is very distressing for me to have to go back through all this. Are we nearly finished?'

'Just a few more questions, so that I am fully informed,' Wilfrid smiled. 'Would it have been possible for Tyrrell to have taken an arrow from the king's quiver?'

'Almost certainly, since he was behind him in the moments prior to the arrow being loosed.'

'And yet you told me only a few moments ago that you are unable to recall whether Tyrrell was ahead of Rufus, or behind him, when the arrow was fired. And since it pierced the king's chest, it must be assumed that Tyrrell was well in front of Rufus, and turned in order to loose the arrow. Could he not have walked past the king, taking an arrow from his quiver as he did so, then turned and let fly that arrow?'

'I suppose it could have happened as you suggest.'

'Did anyone think to count how many arrows were left in Rufus's quiver?'

'No, since it seemed obvious that it must have been one of Tyrrell's.'

'And where is Walter Tyrrell now?'

'On his estates in Poix-de-Picardie, near Amiens, in northern France. He fled there immediately after the king died, and he was joined by his wife and children a few weeks later.'

'His wife is your sister, is she not?'

'That's correct — my sister Adeliza.'

'And where lies this estate of his in relation to the Norman estates of Duke Robert?'

'Just to the north of them, why?'

'Duke Robert would therefore be perfectly placed to grant Tyrrell sanctuary and protection from any retribution that King Henry might seek for the loss of a brother.'

Gilbert laughed harshly and gave Wilfrid a disbelieving stare. 'I doubt if either of the remaining brothers will be mourning the loss of William Rufus.'

'Why did you abandon his body?'

The lingering smile was wiped instantly from Gilbert's face. 'We didn't. We made haste to return to the hunting lodge, along with the remainder of the hunting party that was some quarter of a mile behind us. We gave orders that an urgent message be relayed to Winchester, in order that the king's body might be transported with all dignity back to the palace there.'

'Was the person to whom that order was given not punished for his laxity?'

'Why should they have been?'

'I think you know why, Earl Gilbert. The body was brought back — eventually — on a handcart by two forest peasants who had discovered it. That was several days later, by which time England had a new king.'

'What are you accusing me of?'

'Nothing. I will simply be making a report to King Henry, as he requested. We shall take our leave on the morrow, but forgive me if I politely decline any invitation to go hunting with you this afternoon.'

Wilfrid walked outside deep in thought, a terrible idea forming in his mind. The version of events he had just received from Gilbert de Clare was strikingly different from the one given by King Henry. One of them was either lying, or simply mistaken in their attempt to remember, several months after the event, the details of an incident that by any standard must have been sudden, confused, emotional and violent. He would need to acquire other recollections of the same tragedy, and the obvious next place to enquire was well north of London. But before things got any more confused in his mind, he needed to record the differences in some sort of document for ease of recall when he presented his final report to King Henry. Or perhaps he would be shrinking from that task when the time came, because in one version of events he might well be revealing suspicions that it would not be convenient to reveal, to the person who least wanted to hear them.

He looked unseeingly across the outer keep, and only after a few moments did he become aware that his daughter Matilda was deep in conversation with a liveried man at arms who was lounging against a wall. Remembering how easy it had been for him to engage the interest of a royal serving girl all those years ago, Wilfrid walked swiftly towards them. The man looked up as he saw Wilfrid approaching, and said something to Matilda, who turned and smiled.

'Father,' she announced as he drew level with them. 'This man is named Howard, and he has family in Suffolk, where the de Clare family also own estates.'

'Very nice for him, I'm sure,' Wilfrid replied with a forced smile, 'but if "Howard" would excuse us, I have need of you inside. Good-day, young man.'

As he steered Matilda towards the main castle building, she protested mildly, 'That was blunt to the point of rudeness, Father. We were only talking.'

Wilfrid stopped, obliging her to do likewise. 'Show me your hands,' he demanded.

She did so. 'No chainmail marks, have no fear.'

'This is good. Not because I did not want you being too familiar with a common soldier, but because I need your fair hand in full working order. When we go back inside, I shall call for writing implements, and I will tell you what I need to have recorded.'

Shortly before supper was served, Matilda had written down, with several frowns, the brief points dictated to her by her father. Wilfrid's brows remained knitted while he dictated the discrepancies between the two accounts he had received of the circumstances surrounding the death of King William Rufus. They were short but telling.

Henry had recalled that the group of which he had been a part — along with Gilbert and Roger Clare — was slightly ahead of the second group of Rufus and Tyrrell, off to their right. Gilbert's version of events put his party slightly behind.

Gilbert had also recalled Henry being in the lead of his party, whereas Henry had made no mention of that telling point.

Whoever had been in the lead would, if Henry's version was correct, have been well placed to turn to his right and loose a fatal shot at Rufus, since — according to Henry's account — the entire party had been slightly in front of Rufus's.

Was Gilbert trying to conceal the fact that Henry had acquired the crown of England by murdering his own brother? If so, why had he been prepared to suggest that Henry might have been leading his party? Would it not have been more consistent to claim that someone else — himself or his brother Roger — had been in the best position to loose off a shot?

Then there was the matter of Rufus trying to pull the arrow from his chest. Both Gilbert and Henry had made mention of that, although Henry only in passing. But Gilbert's explanation for knowing of it was far from convincing. It might only have been obvious to whoever broke into the right-hand clearing immediately after the firing of the fatal arrow and Rufus's scream of pain, and if that person had been Gilbert, did it not suggest that he had been in the lead position in the left-hand party, and not Henry? Did Henry's knowledge come from what he was told after the event by Gilbert? An alternative explanation was that Gilbert had seen the entire incident, including Rufus's attempt to extract the arrow, and knew that the shot had been loosed by Henry. This might also account for his current favoured status.

Neither Henry nor Gilbert had described any conversation immediately before Tyrrell fled, and there might not have been any. Significantly, Gilbert had also said nothing about a conversation in which Henry was urged to lose no time in claiming the throne, although Henry had mentioned it without disclosing any of the details. Was Henry lying on that point, or had Gilbert simply forgotten to mention it? If no such conversation had taken place, it certainly made Henry's actions seem all the more callous and opportunistic, and it suited Henry to maintain the impression that he had needed to be persuaded.

Finally, the abandoning of the body. There could be no blame attached to Henry for that, since he had ridden hard to Winchester, either on his own initiative or on the urgings of others. But Gilbert and Roger? By now, they would have had ample opportunity to bribe someone to admit dereliction of duty in not making arrangements for the body to be treated with all the respect it deserved, so there was nothing to be gained from that source. But the fact was that the body had lain undetected for as long as it took for Henry to set in train his own hasty accession — had he ordered that, and had the Gilbert brothers simply gone along with it? Or was it solely their idea once Henry had ridden off, and if so — why? What, if anything, were they seeking to hide? Did they simply wish their brother-in-law Tyrrell to have more time to make his escape?

After supper, Wilfrid yawned as his head spun. Joan looked at him anxiously.

'We've all had a long day, and you tell us that we will be leaving after breakfast tomorrow, although you didn't say where to,' she said. 'We should all sleep while we can, so that we'll look more refreshed when we get back to Walsingham.'

Wilfrid yawned again. 'That may be a while yet. Tomorrow we head to Hertford, and, I suspect, more lies.'

XX

Thomas looked out of the upper storey window of his guest room in Blois Palace as he heard the unmistakeable sound of a sizeable horse-borne retinue approaching the front gate. He couldn't quite make out who they were, since the massive gate obscured his view, but he was hopeful — without any logical reason — that it might be Emma and her entourage returning from Bayonne, wherever that might be. Whoever was seeking admission was clearly welcome, since the gate swung open within seconds, and Thomas was reminded of the less than generous response to his own return two days ago.

He looked down and recognised the unmistakable form of Henri D'eauville, one of Duke Robert's trusted captains. He was over six feet in height and was missing one ear — according to legend, he had donated it to the former residents of Jerusalem on his way in. Beside him was the more ferrety Gaston Lumiere, his second in command. He was an English speaker who was one of the few Normans who had deigned to address Thomas and Geoffrey in their native language during long nights by campfires in the deserts of Anatolia. They were heavily armed, and over their chainmail they proudly sported the livery surcoats of Normandy, which arrogantly replicated those of England, as if they claimed suzerainty over it.

Thomas sighed and made plans to leave after daybreak. He opted to reward himself with liberal quantities of the local *vin de pays* in compensation for the churlish way in which he had been treated on his return. Consequently, the sun was high in the sky before an usher succeeded in shaking him awake with the information that the breakfast that had been left for him two hours earlier was beginning to curl on the platters.

It was the middle of the day by the time he pointed his horse northward, not even giving Blois the courtesy of a backward glance, and by sunset he was barely fifteen miles into his delayed return to England. There was an auberge ahead on his left, and he was about to nudge his horse into its spacious front yard when he noticed the handful of men at arms sitting at a crude table in front of the hostelry, swigging what was presumably strong beer. There was a movement in the doorway, and a rousing cheer from the men outside heralded the appearance of Gaston Lumiere, accompanied by two serving girls carrying more pots of ale.

This was a typical wayside scene on a late autumn afternoon, except that Gaston and his men were no longer wearing Norman livery. They had each been supplied with surcoats of blue and grey that identified them as servants of Blois, and the first loud toast was to the downfall of 'fat Henry who murdered his brother, but who will be avenged by the rightful heir to England. God defend Duke Robert of Normandy!'

Thomas kept his horse at a steady pace as he ambled past the group, and only urged him on harder once he was safely beyond them and further down the road that led to Cherbourg.

Little wonder that Duke Stephen had not wished him to remain in Blois for too long, or to convey any further message to King Henry. Thomas now had a message of his own to impart, and urgently.

Duke Robert of Normandy rose to meet the man whose entrance had just been announced, and with one welcoming arm around his shoulder he guided him to the seat next to the throne, ordering that the new arrival be served with wine.

'Ranulf, my old friend, it is *so* good to see that you remain in one piece. Did my wimp of a younger brother treat you harshly during your imprisonment?'

Flambard grinned with the boyish charm that had so captivated the now deceased Rufus as he shook his head. 'Henry remains as soft as ever, and ordered that I be treated with respect, given that I had served his brother so loyally. He even gave instruction that I be fed. It didn't seem to occur to him that I had been robbing the Treasury blind for all those years, and could well afford to have a banquet brought in every night, had I so chosen. The guards at the Tower all seemed to be new to the king's service, and were easily bribed. From there it was but two days' hard ride to Dover, and I was in Calais before my absence was even noted. Henry's weakness of spirit will be his undoing — that, and his lust for women.'

'We may use each of those to our advantage, ere long,' Robert nodded. 'But how have his subjects accepted him?'

'Most were taken unawares by the speed with which he seized the crown. Even though Archbishop Anselm was safely over here under your protection, Henry bullied the Bishop of London into doing the job. The common people are probably unaware that they even have a new king, and most of them will be indifferent when they *do* learn. Regarding the nobles, my money will probably erase any remaining value they place on loyalty, given that many of them have lands over here that you can confiscate, should they not rally to your banner. When do you expect to invade?'

'Next spring, if all goes well. We have plans afoot to seize the Treasury a few days beforehand, plans that are in the hands of my brother-in-law Stephen of Blois. He has a long-standing grievance with Henry over some land on the borders of Cotentin, and needed little persuasion. He has men of mine, disguised as men of his, who will scout the land immediately inland from Portsmouth, on the south coast west of Winchester. He is doing all this under pretence of a marriage treaty between one of his daughters and the new Treasurer Herbert of Winchester. What kind of man is he?'

Ranulf sneered. 'A mild-mannered fool who does what he is told by Henry, and cannot believe his good fortune in being appointed Treasurer. But once he is disposed of, there are many inside the Treasury who will welcome a return to the old days, in which a fair share of the royal income never quite made it into the strong boxes. But is Stephen prepared to sacrifice one of his daughters to an old man like Herbert? He is well past forty, to judge by his white hair and paunch. He is also deeply religious, and therefore boring — what unfortunate princess of Blois has to pretend to feel affection for him until the trap has been sprung?'

'Fortune even smiles on us in that regard, it would seem,' Robert grinned. 'Countess Adela, our sister, has ever disapproved of Stephen's bastard daughter, Emma. Adela has persuaded him that if he wants a peaceful life without her carping voice in his ear, Emma must be sacrificed for the general good. Emma is said to be quite comely, so that will be some consolation to old Herbert before he is done to death by one of her retinue, which will of course be generously supplied with assassins.'

'Has Henry accepted?'

'He has little choice. Since he has not married, he has no legitimate children of his own to offer in a marriage treaty. It would have been an insult to offer a mere Treasurer to a lady of the true blood, so the offer of Emma was a perfect arrangement for both sides.'

'Has anyone bothered to consult the lady in question?'

'Is that a serious question, Ranulf, or have you grown soft during your time in the Tower that Rufus built, little knowing that his true love would one day occupy it?'

'Enough of that,' Flambard blushed. 'But the answer to your question is "no". I have not grown soft — merely vengeful.'

XXI

'I suppose we'll reach home eventually,' Joan muttered disparagingly as she tested the bolster on the bed that all but filled their narrow chamber in Hertford Castle. The fortress was a poor imitation of the one they had recently left; it was still a wooden structure on a mound of earth, like all those originally constructed on the orders of the Norman invader a generation earlier. However, given that its overlord Roger de Clare did not possess the wealth of his older brother Gilbert, it had not yet made the conversion into stone that most other Norman castles were undergoing. As a result, it was draughty and smelt of old soil, which no number of rich hangings and rushes on the bare floors could eliminate.

Roger de Clare at least had a title under which to conceal his relative poverty, and he took himself very seriously, like all younger brothers who lived in the shade of an older sibling. He received Wilfrid with a haughty disdain that hid his unease, because the two brothers might well lose a great deal if the truth came out, and this middle-aged man with the commission from Henry seemed determined to unearth it.

'Why would King Henry wish to learn more of the unfortunate circumstances of his brother's death, since he was present at it?' Roger enquired suspiciously, as he indicated the chair in which Wilfrid was invited to sit. It was two feet below the raised platform on which Roger sat — a clear signal that he regarded himself as being above this mere messenger.

Wilfrid smiled disarmingly as he noted Roger's unease. 'Clearly King Henry only saw part of what happened. He hopes, as the result of my enquiries, to obtain as much information as possible, given that there are those who now accuse him of being the one who loosed the shot. Or, at least, the one who commanded it.'

'I can assure you that neither of those outrageous accusations is true,' Roger replied assertively, but with a slight tremble in his voice.

'I am of course reassured to hear that,' Wilfrid oozed, 'but since you speak with such assurance, presumably you clearly saw what *did* happen.'

'It was difficult to see anything,' Roger replied defensively, 'since there was a bright sunset that evening, and we were blinded by it.'

'So your brother advises me,' Wilfrid replied.

Roger looked even more uncomfortable. 'You have spoken with my brother? What account did he give of the tragedy?'

'Simply that he saw nothing, but believed that you might have seen more of what happened,' Wilfrid lied.

'I probably saw no more than he did,' Roger asserted.

'But presumably no *less*, so tell me what you remember.'

Roger crossed his legs — a sure sign of a man ill at ease, Wilfrid reminded himself — and began a hesitant description of the incident. 'We had divided into two groups. Rufus insisted on being accompanied by Walter Tyrrell, since he was the most skilled with the bow, and we were desirous of having venison for dinner the following day. They went off along a track to the right, and we took the left path.'

'In what order?' Wilfrid enquired. 'Those of you on the left path — who was in the lead, and how were the other two disposed?'

Roger closed his eyes and thought before replying. 'My brother Gilbert was in the lead. I seem to recall that this was the case, since Henry and I dropped back slightly to discuss our prospects of success in the hunt, given that the light was blinding us. Henry was slightly ahead of me, but only by a foot or so. It was a narrow track, and we were proceeding stealthily.'

'But there is no doubt, in your memory, that Gilbert was ahead of you both?'

'No doubt at all. Then there was a noise to our right in the undergrowth, and something broke cover. I believe that it was a stag that we had startled, and it headed away from us.'

'The bright sunlight did not prevent you seeing that?'

'The sunlight came only from directly in front, and it was possible to see to either side.'

'So you would have had a clear view of Rufus and Walter to your right?'

'Yes and no. There was a lot of high vegetation at that point, but they were visible from time to time as they moved forward at roughly the same pace as ourselves.'

'Your brother recalled that the paths were running at an equal distance from each other, and not diverging,' Wilfrid lied, in order to test his growing belief that the brothers had agreed a story between them, but had not quite rehearsed the finer points.

'That's correct,' Roger confirmed. 'We could see them quite clearly though the occasional gaps in the vegetation.'

'And who was in the lead — Rufus or Walter?'

Roger's hesitation seemed to reveal another fine point on which the brothers had failed to agree, but he finally spoke with what sounded like certainty. 'Walter, most definitely. Once the deer — or whatever it was — broke cover, I believe that Rufus loosed a shot at it, but only wounded it, and Walter shouted something like "Leave it to me, sire", and moved ahead with his bow pulled back, presumably intending to finish the beast off.'

'What happened next?'

'We heard Rufus yell out in pain. Through the undergrowth, I could see that he was attempting to pull an arrow from his chest. Then he fell to the ground, and we all rushed over.'

'You are certain in your mind that you did not move to your right until *after* you had seen Rufus with the arrow in his chest?'

'Quite certain.'

'And Walter Tyrrell remained ahead of him?'

'Not ahead — to the side.'

'But he had been ahead of Rufus immediately before the fatal arrow was fired?'

'Yes. That was why we were so certain that he must have fired the shot.'

'But for the entire period of that few seconds that you claim to have been looking to your right, you had them both in your sight?'

'Yes.'

'But you didn't see Walter fire any arrow — either at an animal, or at Rufus?'

'No.'

'So when Walter was accused of the death, whether by accident or otherwise, why did you not speak in his defence?'

'It was the arrow,' Roger replied, clearly ruffled. 'The arrow that came from Walter's quiver.'

'This is the first I have heard of an arrow, apart from the one that finished up in the king's chest,' Wilfrid lied again, certain that he was being fed badly rehearsed falsehoods.

'There was an arrow — or at least, part of an arrow,' Roger hastened to explain, as if this would resolve the issue. 'It was lying to the king's side, and was clearly the one he had attempted to remove, but he had only succeeded in snapping it off. It had a gold fletching, and it was one of those given to Walter only that morning.'

'By whom?'

'The royal archer — Giles Montferrat.'

'Why would the royal archer give arrows to a mere nobleman?'

'Forgive me, I digress. He actually gave six of them to the king, and the king made a gift of two of them to Walter, since he was the best archer of all of us.'

'So the king had four of his own?'

'Correct.'

'So how can you be certain that the fatal arrow wasn't one of his?'

'Why would Rufus shoot himself? And for that matter — how?'

'It could have been taken from his quiver.'

'That was not possible,' Roger assured him. 'We examined the king's quiver, and there were three arrows left in it. Given that he had loosed one into the beast, that accounted for the four he had retained. But there was one missing from Tyrrell's quiver.'

'Did you confront him with that fact?'

'Of course, and he could give no explanation. Then he ran, thereby leaving no doubt regarding his guilt.'

'He was not urged to run?'

'No, he just took off.'

'There were others in the hunting party, apart from the five of you?'

'Indeed — foresters, royal bodyguards, grooms and suchlike, but they were well behind us, and none of them could have fired that shot.'

'My point was to enquire why none of you saw fit to raise the hue and cry, and demand the arrest of the man who had just killed the king.'

Roger had no answer to that, and merely shook his head.

'And what of Henry?'

'Meaning?'

'What was his reaction to what had just transpired?'

'He ran off also.'

'There was no conversation before he ran?'

'None. But we heard later, on our return to the hunting lodge, that he had ridden to Winchester and taken command of the Treasury that is kept there. A few days later he rode to London, where he was crowned king.'

'And what of the dead king's body?'

'We gave orders that it was to be removed by those who accompanied us, to the hunting lodge.'

'Not directly to the royal place at Winchester?'

'No.'

'But not even that order was obeyed, was it?'

'Unfortunately not. The body was not brought into the palace until four days later, the arrow head still embedded in it. It was beginning to smell by that time.'

'And those who brought it in were local peasants?'

'So I was advised.'

'You have been very patient with me, Earl Roger, for which I am greatly indebted to you,' Wilfrid assured him. 'I have only one matter left to enquire about.'

'Ask away,' Roger invited him as he appeared to relax.

'Your eyes were to the right during the crucial moment when Rufus received the arrow in his chest?'

'Correct.'

'But you did not see Tyrrell fire it?'

'Also correct.'

'From which direction did it come?'

'I beg your pardon?'

'The arrow — did it hit Rufus from his right or from his left?'

'I cannot be certain — his back was to me at the time. As I already mentioned, there was a good deal of vegetation that obscured the view.'

'So it could have come from the king's left?'

'Yes — I suppose it could.'

'From somewhere ahead of you?'

Roger's face froze in horror when he finally saw the corner he had talked himself into. 'Yes, but…'

'But what?'

'There was no-one ahead of me.'

'According to what you told me earlier, your brother Gilbert was ahead of you.'

'That was earlier,' Roger replied weakly.

'Had he rejoined you and Henry by that point?'

'I — I cannot be certain.'

'Of course not,' Wilfrid grinned with satisfaction. 'Forgive me, I had forgotten — your eyes were to the right the entire time, as you already advised me. You couldn't have seen what was happening ahead of you, could you?'

'No.'

'So there could have been someone ahead of you, to the king's left, who could have fired the fatal shot?'

'Yes — I suppose so, but it wasn't my brother.'

'How can you be certain, since you saw nothing of what was happening ahead of you on the left track?'

'I don't think I like what you're implying,' Roger asserted feebly.

'I'm simply piecing the events together from what you were able to tell me.'

'Will you be reporting all this to King Henry?'

'I would be a poor royal commissioner if I did not,' Wilfrid reminded him. 'What time do you serve supper?'

'Why could we not at least have stayed for supper?' Joan demanded as they trotted line abreast up the slight rise that took them south out of Hertford.

'The answer to that question depends upon whether or not you wished to take the risk of being poisoned,' Wilfrid advised her. 'Although that would have been far preferable to having us hacked to death in our beds.'

'I think I prefer the quiet life in Walsingham after all,' Matilda announced with a shudder. 'Is it always like this in the king's service?'

'Why do you think I prefer the crop fields of home rather than the treachery of life at court?' Wilfrid asked. 'Hopefully all this has driven from your mind any ambition to wed a wealthy earl who might leave you a wealthy widow within two years of marriage.'

'Why must you always make your point more than once?' Matilda grumbled.

'And perhaps you would now like to make a point about where we will spend the night,' Joan added. 'It looks like rain up ahead, and I need to wash.'

'On our journey here earlier today,' Wilfrid replied, 'I saw at least three abbeys. I had not expected that we would need to prevail upon their hospitality quite so soon, but neither did I expect my meeting with Roger de Clare to turn out the way it did. Now, I must speak urgently with the king, and if we rise early tomorrow, we may be in Westminster by sunset.'

Two days later, Wilfrid was admitted to the royal presence, instructed to take a seat, and offered wine.

'I had not expected you back so soon,' said King Henry. 'I take it that you have something to impart?'

'Indeed I have, sire, but if you would forgive me, there are certain additional questions I must ask of you before I disclose what I have learned, and what I have deduced from that.'

'If you must, but make it brief.'

'The party you were with, the party that took the left path. Who was in the lead?'

'Gilbert de Clare. I remember that well enough, since I was using his large body ahead of me to block out some of the sunlight.'

'And where was his brother Roger?'

'Behind me, as I recall. I was puffing hard to keep up with Gilbert and his lengthy strides, and Roger kept treading on my heels in his enthusiasm to get ahead.'

'And the group to your right, containing the king. Was it possible to keep them in view for the whole time?'

'Of course not. We were in the densest part of the forest, and the bracken must have been six feet high. In addition, the trees grew thickly at that point — elms, I believe they were.'

'And after the discovery of the body, Walter Tyrrell did not run off immediately?'

'No, he stayed to protest his innocence. It was only after the discovery of his arrow that Gilbert persuaded him to flee. Perhaps he was unwise to take that advice.'

'Indeed, he may well have been, sire,' Wilfrid announced, 'since I believe that your brother was deliberately shot, by one of the de Clare brothers — probably Gilbert.'

'What leads you to that belief?'

'They tell suspiciously different stories, both designed to deflect suspicion from themselves. After this length of time, one might expect slight differences in recollection, but they give different accounts of matters that should be well within their memories, such as who was positioned where in the left-hand group of which you were a member, and whether or not Tyrrell was urged to flee.'

'They deny that?' Henry enquired, wide-eyed. 'That sticks out clearly in my memory, principally because Gilbert was screaming at him to run while he could, while Walter seemed reluctant to go, as if somehow his innocence was beyond question.'

'The behaviour of an innocent man?'

'Precisely. But why would the Gilbert brothers desire my brother's death? He had been generous to a fault with them, and if anyone had cause to be grateful for the mercy of my treacherous brother, it was those two.'

'I have given that point considerable thought, sire. Is it possible that what they wished to bring about was not the king's death, but Walter's blame for it?'

'Why would they wish that? He's married to their sister.'

'Perhaps the answer lies in some family dispute. I must at some stage cross to Normandy, in order to speak with Tyrrell himself, and perhaps his wife. But first I must interview the Royal Fletcher, Giles Montferrat.'

Henry sighed. 'He retired from my service, at his own request, shortly after your recent departure. It was unexpected, and I have since learned that he is to be found on his estate somewhere around Lincoln. He must have lived frugally while here at Westminster, since the pension I granted him would not have bought him an estate of his own. A humble cottage on the estate of another, perhaps, but not an entire estate.'

'Does it not occur to you that he may have been bribed or threatened?'

'And why would that be?'

'He must know something about the arrows he supplied to Rufus earlier that day.'

'You may be right. What the devil is that racket outside?'

Two men could be heard arguing on the other side of the heavy door to the chamber in which they sat. One of the voices — louder and more insistent than the other — was very familiar to Wilfrid's ears. He rose from his chair and began to walk down the chamber, just as the door burst open and two men tumbled in.

'Forgive me, sire — he overpowered me, and I am not armed,' the usher blurted out. 'Perhaps Sir Wilfrid could draw his weapon and assist?'

Wilfrid's face broke into a smile. 'I have never drawn a weapon against my own son, except during arms training, so why would I do so now?' He ran the last few feet towards Thomas and lifted him off his feet with an embrace.

'No need for introductions, clearly,' said Henry. He dismissed the usher with a reassurance that he would not be held responsible for the unauthorised entry, provided that he brought more wine immediately, together with an additional goblet. 'If the family reunion is completed,' Henry continued as he waved Thomas to another chair, 'perhaps you would explain the reason for your forced entry into the royal chamber, for which the last King of England would have removed your head.'

'Sire!' Thomas panted. 'I fear that there is a plot against your throne!'

'There are plots against the throne of England every week these days,' Henry replied dryly. 'It was so in my father's day, and also in my brother's. So what is so different on this occasion?'

'This comes from just across the Channel, sire. I was in Blois, as you requested, and I delivered your response to the offer of a peace treaty. But I was not made to feel welcome, and Count Stephen seemed anxious for me to depart without bearing any further message for you. A few days later, after I had delayed my departure, I think I discovered the reason. A squadron of armed men dressed in the livery of Normandy clattered in, and I recognised two of their leaders. The following day, they rode out again and headed through the Cotentin towards Cherbourg, dressed as if they were men of Blois. I was able to ride ahead, and saw them take ship for Portsmouth — so I was told by the captain of the sister vessel, which was due to sail for Dover later that day. I was able to obtain passage, and from Dover I rode hard here. That was two days ago, and the Normans in disguise will no doubt be in Portsmouth by now, wreaking havoc.'

'How many men, would you estimate?' Wilfrid enquired.

'Thirty at most, that I saw anyway.'

Wilfrid shook his head as he framed his reply. 'Thirty men would not make it beyond the harbour. More likely they are spying out the town's defences for some sort of future armed landing.'

'It is probably as you advise,' Henry nodded, 'but already they have sought safe passage to London, in the name of the Count of Blois, to parley with me regarding which of the peace proposals I put to Stephen he has accepted. I ordered the Governor of Portsmouth to let them through with an escort along the London road.'

'They mean to assassinate you!' Thomas warned him. 'I fought alongside some of them in the Crusade, and they are skilled swordsmen — desperate characters no doubt sent by Blois to do away with you.'

'That is a risk I must run,' Henry insisted. 'You may well be right to sniff a plot from Normandy. My brother Robert has let it be known that he disputes my right to rule England, and Ranulf Flambard escaped some weeks ago from the Tower. He is believed to have sought sanctuary at Robert's court, and he will no doubt have much to advise Robert regarding the current state of our army.'

'Then why allow these invaders hospitality at your court?' Thomas demanded, horrified.

Henry smiled reassuringly. 'I cannot refuse them, if they bring confirmation that England and Blois will be joined by treaty. Stephen needs protection against Robert on his eastern border, and it is in both our interests to maintain the Cotentin as a safe route between England and France.'

'What are the terms of this proposed treaty, if I might enquire?' Wilfrid asked.

Henry shrugged. 'That is why I must meet with these emissaries from Blois. I offered Stephen a choice, and those who are approaching London are no doubt carrying his decision.'

'What was that choice?'

'One of them was marriage for myself. I do not yet have a wife, and Stephen suggested several ladies of his court. I replied with a suggestion that perhaps a cousin of his, or even one of the more noble ladies of his court, might like to marry our own Treasurer, Herbert of Winchester. He is hugely wealthy in his own right, and unmarried. I am considering moving the Treasury to a safe vault under the Tower that my brother Rufus built, since it seems more secure.'

'It may well be that these visitors from across the sea have a double purpose, sire,' Wilfrid pointed out, 'and their second purpose may not even be fully known to Count Stephen. But it might be more diplomatic to take them at face value, and discuss the treaty proposals with them.'

'That's rubbish, Father!' Thomas protested, before stopping and apologising for his disrespect. 'If Count Stephen merely intended to talk peace treaties, he would have sent his reply through me. And if he means his Majesty ill, what is more convenient than to use Normans who can be blamed if something goes wrong with their plot on his life?'

'Your concern for my welfare is both touching and welcome,' said Henry. 'Will you remain and take up a senior armed role in my household? "Constable of Westminster", perhaps? Or "Royal Chamberlain"? And what of you, Sir Wilfrid? Might such a title appeal to you?'

Father and son shook their heads in unison. Thomas spoke first.

'I will gladly return to your service here in Westminster, sire. But first I have a personal reason for wishing to return to my family's estate in Walsingham.'

'As do I,' Wilfrid added with an enquiring sideways glance at his son.

Henry nodded. 'I quite understand. You both have my leave to depart, and I thank you for your loyal service to me already. But do not forget to return as soon as is convenient — *both* of you. And I would be further obliged if you could return at the head of an army.'

As they left the chamber, Wilfrid turned to Thomas. 'Your mother and sister will be both surprised and delighted to find you here in London. But what is this "personal reason" you have for returning to Walsingham?'

'Ah, well, Father,' Thomas smiled, 'you see, there was this lovely lady…'

XXII

Wilfrid, Joan, Matilda and Thomas returned to find the Manor of Walsingham in deep mourning, a freshly dug grave mound a few feet away from the entrance to the shrine, and a convent with a new Mother Superior. As they sat round the supper table on their first night home, Geoffrey de Faverches brought them up to date with all that had been happening in their absence.

'It was obvious that Mother was fading fast,' he explained, 'but, typically, she would listen to no-one in her enthusiasm to ensure that all was as it should be. She was often out of breath, and complaining of pains in her chest, and then one morning Sister Grace found her lying face-down in front of the statue, her life gone from her, but a wonderful aura of peace around her body. The new Abbot of Ely, Abbot Richard, was summoned, and he came, along with Elston, to conduct the burial service with full rites.'

'And Aunt Elva has replaced her?' Matilda prompted him.

'Could anyone be surprised at that?' Geoffrey smiled as Elva looked down modestly at the table and quietly made the sign of the Cross. 'Abbot Richard gathered all the convent congregation around him and explained that it was customary for those who had taken their final vows to elect their next Holy Mother. There are currently only three of them, apart from Elva, and Mother had always let it be known that she was her preferred successor. She is also greatly loved and respected, so before the abbot left we had a new "Mother Grace". She claims that nothing has changed, and that she does not feel the burden of office hanging heavily upon her, but all the same I'm sure she welcomes the return of Tilly, particularly with regard to the orphanage. It has grown considerably in the past year or so, and now has fourteen children aged from ten downwards.'

'If you still want to take the veil, you would be very welcome,' Elva beamed across at her niece, whose glance dropped down to the food before her.

'During our recent travels, Tilly has learned that young men come in more attractive shapes and sizes than can be found on a Norfolk estate,' Wilfrid explained.

Matilda's blush confirmed that point, but Mother Grace was not to be deterred.

'Even without the veil, I really need you to take over the orphanage if I am to properly discharge all my other duties.'

'And I'd be delighted,' Matilda confirmed. Then, with a sideways glance at Thomas, she added, 'I may even be able to add to the numbers.'

The following morning, Wilfrid and Thomas stood with Geoffrey at the top of the slope that ran down from the manor house to the river.

'How well prepared are the men?' Wilfrid enquired.

Geoffrey shrugged. 'They're fit enough. I made sure of that upon my return. But we won't know if they're any good at all the fighting techniques I've tried to instil in them until they face a real enemy. Perhaps "*Sir* Thomas" here can take them back on crusade.'

Before Thomas could react to this fresh outbreak of rivalry, Wilfrid intervened. 'He may well get an opportunity to test them before long. The new King Henry is in urgent need, both of an army to oppose a threatened invasion from Normandy, and a smaller contingent to guard his person, for reasons that Thomas can explain. I propose that once the harvest is in, he takes twenty of our best men down to London with him, in a revival of the old "housecarl" system.'

'I heard tell of them from my mother, but never really understood their true function,' Geoffrey frowned.

'You don't *need* to know, do you, since you won't be leading them?' Thomas reminded him.

'What Thomas means,' Wilfrid explained diplomatically, 'is that you, Geoffrey, will have the equally important task of raising a new army that we can take to the nation's defence against the threatened invasion. You'll be left with a hard core here on the estate, and can pick up more men as you march wherever the mood takes you. Think of it as a sort of human snowball, growing bigger the further it rolls. Hopefully, by the time you reach London, it will have grown to five thousand.'

Geoffrey raised his eyebrows. 'Will you be joining me in this recruitment drive? And you still haven't told me what "housecarls" were.'

'They were an elite group of warriors whose only function was to guard the king's person,' Thomas advised him, puffing out his chest. 'Father served as one to the last Saxon king, Harold.'

'*My* father, you mean?' Geoffrey smirked back at him.

Wilfrid realised that, as her days were drawing to a close, Geoffrey's mother had left him in no doubt of his true heritage. 'As for your question regarding my leading your army,' he added hastily before Thomas could think of a suitable retort, 'my days as a warrior are over, or at least I hope so. It's time for the next generation to take up the reins of leadership, and we have nurtured two of the best here at Walsingham.'

'When do you wish me to leave?' Thomas asked reluctantly.

'Have you grown too accustomed to home comforts again already?' Wilfrid teased. 'The sooner you pick your men and head south, the sooner King Henry will be protected from those imposters sent from Blois — or was it Normandy? Either way, you should leave without delay once the last of the harvest is in.'

'Mother will not be pleased,' Thomas frowned.

'She never is, these days, but blame me for that.'

Neither of them were proved wrong when Joan protested loudly at her only son being sent back to London on what sounded like a dangerous mission.

'We don't know for certain that it's dangerous,' Wilfrid attempted to argue, before being met with the customary snort.

'If the king is not in danger, why are you sending twenty of our best men down to protect him?' she argued. 'And who will guard the estate while he is gone, and Geoffrey is scouring the countryside in search of an army?'

Wilfrid reached out to comfort her. 'That used to be my task, at one time. Or do you fear that I grow too feeble?'

Joan snuggled into him. 'Of course not. All the same, you are leaving the estate more vulnerable by sending its two young leaders away.'

'The estate will be even more vulnerable if Duke Robert is allowed to become our king,' Wilfrid advised her. 'Henry may be overweight, and too fond of books and ladies of the court, but he is, so far as I've been able to judge, the best of the three brothers. While he is safely on the throne, there is more hope for peace here in Walsingham. And that's where I intend to remain, until I'm required. Which hopefully will be never, if Thomas's gloomy warnings turn out to be groundless.'

Wilfrid's optimistic prediction held good for a mere two weeks.

As he sat on a bench outside the manor house in the evening sunset, watching the last of the harvest being garnered, a pony limped in through the manor gateway. On its back was a monk who was recognisable to his uncle even from a distance. Wilfrid rose and welcomed the new arrival.

'Elston, what brings you here again? Not that your presence is unwelcome, but I have a feeling that you bring ill tidings. Sorry — I should of course have addressed you as "Brother Mark". But in either capacity you're still my nephew.'

'Indeed I return as "Brother Mark", with a request for your attendance at Ely,' Elston replied.

'Hopefully there has been no more pillaging of your relics and silverware? I hoped that had ended with the hasty departure from the kingdom of the villainous Ranulf Flambard.'

'No, nothing like that. In fact, possibly nothing at all, except to settle the anxieties of an elderly man who may well be bereft of his wits.'

'Come inside and have some food and drink, then satisfy my curiosity.'

After the usual welcomes, and an invitation from Mother Grace to hear the confessions of her small flock of nuns, which she assured him would not be likely to take more than a few minutes in total, Elston explained the reason for his visit.

'Several days ago, a ragged old man sought sanctuary at the abbey. We took him to be an itinerant beggar of the sort we grant hospitality to with a depressing frequency in these uncertain times. He had bad blisters on his feet, and our infirmarian, Brother Peter, asked me to attend to them. I did so, and stayed briefly to talk to the man, who confided in me that he was in hiding from men who had been sent to threaten him and his family on their estate in Spalding, which is north of here and part of Lincolnshire.'

'Can the lord of his manor not deal with the issue?' Wilfrid asked as he poured them both more wine.

Elston shook his head. 'I had not finished my account. The man *is* the lord of his own manor, according to him, and naturally I asked what had led him to such straits that he had been forced to set out on foot and travel for such a long distance. He claims that those who threatened him and his family also drove off their only two horses, and burned down his barn. I also enquired as to why he had not sought sanctuary in Lincoln itself, and he said that this is where his persecutors had come from, and he dared not venture near there. He then said that he would only be safe if he could seek the sanctuary of the King's Court, since he had information that the king would wish to hear, but which his persecutors were determined to silence. He was actually intent on walking all the way to London by way of hedgerows and ditches. But he claimed to have once been the king's armourer, or something similar, before he retired and took up his estate.'

Wilfrid was suddenly alert. 'Did this man by any chance give the name "Giles Montferrat"?'

'You are obviously known to each other,' Elston replied, 'since he asked me where Sir Wilfrid Walsingham's estate might be located. It seems that your name had been mentioned by those who were threatening his life if he did not remain silent about something that he chose not to disclose to me. However, he had reason to believe that you had been causing trouble for those who sent his assailants to threaten him.'

'Is he still at Ely, or has he already continued on his journey to London?'

'He was still barely able to walk when I left,' Elston assured his uncle, 'so it's unlikely that he's made any further attempt to reach the king. When I advised him that you were my uncle, and that I had been brought up on your estate, the poor man clearly took this as a miracle wrought by God, and pleaded with me to fetch you to him, so I doubt that he will have attempted to move on before I return.'

Three days later, Wilfrid was staring into the frightened eyes of a ragged old man who lay on a cot in the Infirmary of Ely Abbey.

'How do I know I can trust you?' the old man enquired fearfully.

'You believe in God, to the extent of regarding the coincidence of your arrival at the very place from which I could be contacted as some sort of miracle?' Wilfrid challenged him.

'Yes, but how do I know that the monk was not playing me false?'

'That monk is my nephew!' Wilfrid retorted. 'Not only is his mother the Abbess of the Convent of the Holy Sisters of the Blessed Virgin, but his father was my greatest friend. He was killed driving Hereward from the Fens, and I revere his memory. If you can offer me nothing more than insults to my family, then the Devil take you, and good day!'

He moved to rise angrily from the edge of the cot, but as he did so the man grabbed at his wrist with a bony hand still strong from the days when he would tie fletchings to arrow wood.

'Stay! You must forgive me, but I have lately been sorely betrayed by those in whom I thought I could trust.'

'You mean Gilbert and Roger de Clare?'

The old man's face softened slightly. 'You know of them?'

'I have spoken with each of them, and they each told me that you supplied the arrows to King Rufus on the day that he died.'

'Who else was in that party?' Giles enquired, clearly intent on satisfying himself that Wilfrid was not simply bluffing.

'No-one, at the time that the alleged accident occurred, other than the two royal brothers, Rufus and Henry, and the alleged assassin Walter Tyrrell. Except that I believe that it was not an accident, and I have informed our new king of that. If you still suspect my motive for speaking with you, reflect for a moment. You are a weak old man who can barely walk because of your blisters, and I am a seasoned warrior with a sword at my waist. Were I intent on killing you, I would have done so by now, would I not?'

'You may still do so, if I tell you what I know,' the old man croaked.

'You may not need to,' Wilfrid assured him as gently as he was able. 'I have given the matter much thought, and I believe that the fatal arrow was fired on purpose, with intent to kill King William. I believe the person who fired it to have been Gilbert de Clare. And the two brothers, when speaking to me, made much of the fact that the only arrow that was not accounted for was one belonging to Walter Tyrrell. So I suspect that there were other similar arrows, regarding which fact no-one but yourself can confirm. So, as you can deduce, you will be telling me nothing that I do not already suspect — what you *will* be doing is confirming a suspicion that I have already shared with the king.'

The old man's face relaxed slightly. 'I served King William faithfully for his entire reign, and his father before him for three years. I took money for the extra arrows beyond my normal fee for making them, and to my eternal shame I also took their money in return for remaining silent about them after the king's death. Then, as I heard from their bullies when they came after me with their threats, you travelled to each of their castles seeking the truth, and seemed not to believe what you were being told.'

'There *were* more arrows with gold fletchings, you say?' Wilfrid asked.

The old man nodded, his eyes closed. 'Yes, but not until later that day.'

'Tell me the entire tale,' Wilfrid replied encouragingly.

'As they sat at dinner that day, I took a set of six of my best arrows as a gift for the king, to thank him for all the comfortable years I had known in his service. He handed two of them to Master Tyrrell, and kissed him on the cheek. I then withdrew, and shortly afterwards Gilbert came to my workshop and offered me fifty marks if I would make two more exactly the same as the ones I had presented to Rufus, and have them ready to be collected by him by the time that the royal party left for hunting later that day. I was offered a further twenty marks to say nothing of the request, and I regret to admit that took that money as well. My eldest daughter was due to be married to one of the sons of the King's Master of Horse, you see, and we had not at that point been able to save the one hundred marks for her dowry. Then, to ensure my further silence, Roger de Clare gave me one of his minor estates in Lincolnshire — the one they recently raided, with threats that it would all be lost if I opened my mouth to anyone. They even drove off the horses and livestock, and now my only hope for salvation is the king — but I also fear that he may have been the one who commanded the Clare family to do what they did.'

'Thank you very much, Giles,' Wilfrid said as he placed a comforting hand on the man's wrist. 'I shall give word that you are to be hidden securely away here at Ely until it is safe for you to venture abroad again, by which time those who persecute you will have been called to account by King Henry. He, I can assure you, had nothing to do with what happened, and will be only too grateful for you to tell what you know. I shall leave money with Brother Mark for your welfare while you are here.'

XXIII

'You're intending to head off yet again, aren't you?' Joan demanded starchily as she came into the chamber and saw Wilfrid packing clean shirts and hose into a pannier.

He looked up guiltily. 'I intend to join Thomas on his ride to London with the handful of men he has chosen to be the new housecarls to King Henry.'

'They don't all have horses,' Joan reminded him, 'so presumably for most of them it will mean several weeks of trudging the tracks, just as the autumn gales and rain are about to return. Their womenfolk will not thank you, and neither will I.'

'I also have urgent matters to discuss with the king,' Wilfrid added.

'And if you fail to come back, I will also have urgent matters to discuss with you,' Joan threatened, and wondered why Wilfrid had suddenly burst out laughing. Then she realised what she had just said, and despite herself she giggled. Finally the humour turned to tears, and Wilfrid moved quickly across to hold her in his arms.

'Why must it always be like this?' she moaned. 'And who will defend us while you are gone?'

'Geoffrey, until he leaves to recruit an army. I have already instructed him to leave sufficient men behind to guard the estate, and I do not expect to be long away.'

'The last time you assured me of that, you were held in prison for almost two years.'

'That was under a different king,' Wilfrid reminded her. 'It is to prevent that ever happening to anyone else that I ride in support of the new one. Despite his many and obvious weaknesses, he will be a better king than either his father or his older brother.'

Two days later, the advance part of twenty set off south into the bright autumn sunlight, with the usual farewell hugs, kisses, tears, and promises to return. Wilfrid and Thomas rode proudly at their head, and behind them was a wagon commissioned from the manor's mill; this not only contained their armour and other baggage, but also enabled up to half the foot contingent at any time to rest their weary legs. They changed places every five miles or so, and by this means made much swifter progress than they might otherwise have done.

Since the nation was now in a state of comparative peace, they didn't receive fearful stares as they marched through the occasional villages among the flat green pastures, and round the many marshes, of southern Norfolk. The going became even firmer and more direct once they came closer to London, ahead of which the villages became more numerous, and the fields better tended. Two weeks after their departure, they saw the first distant church spire that denoted the northern outskirts of London. The footsteps of the men strengthened as they saw the promised end to their nights camped in fields and hedgerows.

Wilfrid called a halt at an abbey on the western outskirts of the city, in order that the men might wash, rest, and make themselves presentable as an elite group fit to guard a king. There they ate a hearty, if plain, meal prepared for them in the *hospitium* on the instruction of an abbot, who gratefully accepted the handful of coins that Wilfrid slipped to him. Wilfrid and Thomas then stood in the evening sun, listening to the soothing chant of monks engaged in the observance of Vespers in the nearby chapel.

'It wasn't always like this,' Wilfrid said. 'Before you were born, I came through here trailing behind Duke William of Normandy. He'd been refused the bridge access across the Thames by those misguided fools who thought they could thereby prevent his progress. He cut some heads off and planted them on the remains of the bridge, then he marched in a frenzy of revenge all round the countryside until he found a river crossing to the west of here. On his way back east into what is now Westminster, he left very few alive, and the countryside resembled some sort of devastated Hell like the paintings we sometimes see in cathedrals.'

'I forget that you have seen so much,' Thomas replied respectfully. 'It was a wonder that you survived it all. But how can you be certain that the king we ride to protect will be any different? It seems that all these Normans are the same.'

'Spoken like a true Saxon,' Wilfrid chuckled. 'But we must all live with what has happened, and not dream about how it might have been, had Geoffrey's father been victorious in beating off the invaders. As for your question, you forget that I saw all three of the royal brothers when they were mere boys. Robert was noisy and vainglorious, whereas the viciousness of Rufus was obvious even when he was living with the restriction of being a second son. As for our current King Henry, he was quiet and studious, and kept to his chambers for the most part. But he too has his weaknesses, particularly when it comes to women. That may one day be his downfall.'

Thomas remained silent, and Wilfrid sensed that he might have inadvertently struck a sensitive chord in his son's life.

'You never did tell me much about that lady you met across the water who so captured your interest. If you marry her, will she bring you an estate in France, or perhaps a rich dowry?'

Thomas began to search for the words, then decided that this was the appropriate time to be honest. 'She has already brought me a child, father. You have a granddaughter over there. I have only seen her on the one occasion, but she is beautiful, with dark hair and eyes just like her mother's.'

Wilfrid turned to stare at his son in amazement. 'Why did you not tell the rest of the family? Your mother will be *so* delighted.'

'I *did* tell Tilly, because I fear that the child may have to be smuggled into England without anyone knowing of her identity. I had hoped to have her placed in the orphanage on the estate.'

'The lady is already married, you mean?'

'No — at least, not so far as I am aware. But she is high-born, and although her father is aware of what has happened, he did not have me killed. Instead, he has all but banned me from his dukedom.'

'His *dukedom*?' Wilfrid echoed, aghast. 'She is the daughter of Duke Robert? A Norman princess?'

'No — Blois. She's the illegitimate daughter of Count Stephen of Blois, and he is very fond of her.'

Wilfrid's heart sank as he began to contemplate the possible complications that lay ahead of them all, given King Henry's proposed peace treaty with Blois, the general terms of which Thomas was as yet unaware. Somehow, he had to prepare his beloved son for a terrible disappointment. 'Before you arrived in London with news of Duke Robert's possible treachery, the king was advising me that he was close to agreeing the final terms of that peace treaty that you carried with you to Blois. It may involve the arranged marriage of a high-born lady of that nation with one of Henry's own leading courtiers — perhaps his Treasurer.'

'But not a daughter of the count, surely?' Thomas protested, turning pale.

'I don't think that such was being proposed,' Wilfrid reassured him. 'But if the lady is illegitimate, might Count Stephen not be seeking to dispose of her in a gentle way?'

'You may be correct,' Thomas nodded, still ashen-faced. 'The countess heartily disapproves of her presence at the Court of Blois, and although the father dotes on the Lady Emma — that's her name, by the way — it may be that his only way of resolving the conflict is to parcel her off to England. If so, she'll be lost to me.'

'Take heart, Thomas,' Wilfrid replied. 'An illegitimate lady with an illegitimate child of her own is hardly likely to present a good prospect to an English noble. In fact, both he and King Henry might feel insulted by such a proposal. It may be that she will find some way of slipping the child to you in secret, in which case she can be taken back with us to Walsingham.'

'But what of the lady herself?' Thomas moaned, on the point of tears.

Wilfrid was swamped with pity for his son. He placed a comforting hand on his shoulder, and offered the only consolation he could. 'We do not yet know the final details of the peace treaty between England and Blois, if indeed there is to be one. If you are correct, and Duke Robert is planning to invade with assistance from Stephen of Blois, then of course there will be no such treaty — at least not yet. Any such treaty may come at the end of a successful war with Normandy *and* Blois, in which case King Henry will be in a better position to dictate its terms, and it may well be that we can prevail upon him to insist that you be the person betrothed to Lady Emma.'

'That is an awful lot if "ifs", Father,' Thomas replied gloomily. 'But if my only prospect of gaining the lady's hand — along with a legitimate and open claim to custody of my beautiful daughter — is to lead English troops into Normandy and Blois, then so be it.'

'Don't be so eager to throw yourself onto enemy lances,' Wilfrid urged him. 'Your task is to protect King Henry. The duty of collecting, and perhaps leading, his army has been given to Geoffrey, remember.'

'Geoffrey again!' Thomas almost spat. 'We shall see who the king chooses to oppose the enemy at the head of his army.'

'Indeed we shall,' Wilfrid agreed, 'but I would be less than honest if I didn't remind you that both your mother and I would prefer it to be Geoffrey.'

'Do you bring me an army?' King Henry demanded before Wilfrid and Thomas had even finished bowing.

'It follows behind us, sire,' Wilfrid assured him. 'Geoffrey de Faverches, who commands the guard on my estate in Norfolk, is progressing south even as we speak, collecting men as he goes, and we expect him within the month.'

'With how many men?'

'That will rather depend upon how much loyalty there is in the counties around London, sire,' Wilfrid advised him. 'And it may well be that the lords of Clare — the brothers Gilbert and Roger — will be anxious to prove their loyalty in the near future.'

'But why is Sir Thomas here not also recruiting men? If the latest reports I have from Normandy are correct, our southern shores may have been overrun by the time that you have raised your army.'

'My son brings you the best men in Walsingham, sire. They are here as a personal bodyguard for you — what might be termed a "palace guard".'

'I already have one of those,' Henry pointed out grumpily. 'The emissaries from Blois came and went without any untoward incident, so there is no immediate danger to my person.'

'Did you conclude the final terms of a peace treaty?' Wilfrid enquired.

'The final proposed terms went back with the emissaries,' Henry replied, 'and my Treasurer may soon have a wife. Not before time, I would imagine.'

'Do you know who that wife will be?' Thomas blurted, unable to contain his apprehension.

'Did I not just say that the final terms have not been agreed?' Henry replied testily. 'And since your only function around here seems to be protecting my person, rather than querying the terms of my treaties, should you not be about those duties?'

Wilfrid turned quickly, and with a backward jerk of the head instructed Thomas to remove himself from the royal presence. He did so with a somewhat exaggerated bow and a look of distaste. Wilfrid deemed the moment appropriate to divert the king's attention. 'Sire, I believe that I have completed the mission you gave me.'

'What mission? Did I not send you after an army?'

'You did indeed, sire, and might I enquire why there is such a sudden need for it?'

'Because those loyal to me in Normandy have sent word that my brother Robert has moved into Blois with a sizeable army of his own. He has already crossed the borders of my own Cotentin without seeking my leave, which makes me suspect that he has hostile intentions towards England. There are said to be over forty vessels moored in Cherbourg, which by my calculation could carry four thousand fighting men and their horses. That is why I enquired of you regarding the size of our army.'

'Hopefully as much as that, and perhaps more, sire. But what of your other nobles? Have they not pledged to support your cause, should the need arise?'

Henry slumped slightly on his throne. 'I cannot be certain of that, Wilfrid. Robert has spread abroad the wicked lie that I killed my own brother in order to claim the crown of England, and I do not know how many believe that to be true. The Charter of Liberties that I proclaimed at my coronation seems to have placated some of the leading nobles, and Anselm has returned, preaching from his pulpit at Canterbury that it is the Christian duty of every Englishman to fight for the king anointed by God. But other than that, I cannot be sure.'

'What of the brothers Gilbert and Roger de Clare?' Wilfrid enquired.

'What of them? They were great friends of my brother Rufus, of course, and they pledged their allegiance at my coronation, but I'm not sure if they could be prevailed upon to bring men to my battle pennants.'

'What if they were threatened with execution for regicide if they do not, sire?'

Suddenly, Henry's face broke into a broad smile. 'How *could* I have forgotten? Forgive me, it's just that the threat of invasion has completely overtaken my thoughts of late. You have discovered more regarding the death of my brother Rufus?'

'Indeed I have, sire, and I am happy to report that hidden away in the Abbey of Ely is the man who can prove that one or other of them — Gilbert or Roger — did the deed.'

'Are they prepared to admit it?'

'We should perhaps ask them, sire. And in exchange for not having the pair of them separated from their heads, you might add their forces to the army that Geoffrey de Faverches is assembling.'

'Do that, Wilfrid, and do it immediately! You may ride from here on the morrow with arrest warrants for them both. England may yet be saved from another invasion from Normandy!'

XXIV

Gilbert and Roger de Clare were bundled into the royal presence, their hands tied not only at the wrists, but also to each other. Behind each of them were two of Thomas's elite palace guards with drawn swords, prodding them from behind in order to keep them moving forward. On a command from Thomas, they came to a halt, and by pressing each of them on the head in turn, Thomas forced them into a kneeling position in the rushes. They looked up apprehensively to where King Henry sat on his throne with a murderous expression on his face. Beside him sat Sir Wilfrid Walsingham.

'You will remain kneeling until I command you otherwise,' Henry instructed them. 'You will both, of course, remember Sir Wilfrid Walsingham, who recently visited each of you seeking information regarding the unfortunate circumstances in which my brother Rufus met his death. It would seem that you were less than truthful in your answers to him, and he now has further questions. Proceed, Sir Wilfrid.'

'I really have only one further question, should you take this opportunity to be truthful, instead of further wasting my time,' Wilfrid glared at each of them in turn. 'Now, which of you fired the arrow that killed our former king?'

The brothers remained silent, exchanging sidelong glances as if daring the other to speak.

'If I were to advise you that the former Royal Fletcher, Giles Montferrat, is now in a secure place, safely away from your threats on his life, would that assist your memories?'

'Gilbert,' Roger muttered, almost under his breath.

'Bastard!' Gilbert muttered back.

'Louder please, Roger,' Henry commanded.

'Gilbert!' Roger shouted. 'It was Gilbert who loosed the arrow, not me!'

'But you knew he had the arrow in his possession, and what he intended to do with it?' Wilfrid demanded.

It fell silent for a moment until Gilbert shouted, 'Yes, he did! He is as guilty as I.'

'And you will both, of course, be prepared to sign confessions to that effect, as an alternative to having your hands cut off?' Henry demanded in a tone of icy contempt.

Each of the brothers nodded vigorously.

'Any further questions, Sir Wilfrid?'

'Only one, sire, if you would permit me.' He looked back at the two brothers. 'Why did you take the life of your king, who had shown you such favour?'

The brothers exchanged uncomfortable glances, and it was Gilbert who supplied the answer.

'It was a matter of family honour, sire. For some time, the king's chosen bedfellow was Ranulf Flambard, but then he began to show an interest in Walter Tyrrell. Walter is married to our sister Adeliza, and they have several children. Our sister complained to us that Walter was losing his desire for her, and feared that he was conducting an affair with the king, which would be condemned by God and the Church. She pleaded with us to save him from Purgatory, and we tried to persuade Walter away from the king's embraces. But he proclaimed that by submitting to such, he stood to gain much royal favour, and he was also growing to enjoy them. We could not allow that to continue, sire, and so…'

'And so you chose to kill your king, the man to whom you had solemnly sworn allegiance?' Wilfrid thundered.

Henry raised his hand to silence him. 'Even if, for a brief moment, I accept your reason for doing what you did, can you not see that your actions led to half of England believing that I gave the order? I must execute the pair of you for your treasonous act, but I will do so mercifully by the sword if you will each leave behind a sworn confession that may be nailed to the wall of the abbey next door for all to read. If not, you will be boiled alive.'

Roger went green, leaned forward, and vomited into the rushes. To judge by the dark stain that appeared down the front of Gilbert's hose, he had lost control of his bladder.

'Mercy!' Gilbert whined.

'The same mercy you showed to my brother?' Henry enquired in a voice steeled with cold anger. 'Those who commit treason meet with only one end — you must have appreciated that when you did what you did. How do I know you will not plot against my life in the same way?'

'Is there some way in which we can prove our loyalty and preserve our lives, sire?' Gilbert pleaded. Henry pretended to think for a moment, then shook his head, before turning to Wilfrid. 'I can think of nothing, unless Sir Wilfrid has an idea?'

Wilfrid looked hard at each of the brothers in turn. 'How many armed men can you assemble in the king's service, within a month?' he demanded.

'Perhaps five hundred,' Gilbert conceded.

'Three hundred?' Roger croaked hopefully.

'And each of you has left behind a commander, perhaps a Captain of the Guard, or a castellan, who will obey your written instruction?'

Each of them nodded vigorously, and Wilfrid gestured for Henry to take over.

'The man who pushed you into a kneeling position is Sir Thomas Walsingham, son of Sir Wilfrid here,' Henry advised them. 'Each of you will supply him with a written command to your chosen captain to place his men at arms under the command of Sir Thomas, who will bring them here to Westminster. You will remain in the Tower until this process is completed, and if this does not occur within two weeks, you will be tied at your wrists and ankles and thrown into the Thames. Is that understood?'

More vigorous nods preceded the two prisoners being dragged to their feet and marched away. As the chamber door closed behind them, Henry turned to Wilfrid. 'That went well, I think. But get someone to change those rushes, for pity's sake.'

Little more than a week later, Thomas stood proudly on the top step of the entrance to the abbey adjoining the palace, surveying almost a thousand men who stood milling around the yard below him, all dressed in the de Clare livery.

'You are now all soldiers of King Henry,' he shouted above the squawk of the seagulls swirling above the river behind him. 'In due course, you will exchange your current surcoats for those bearing the lions of England. But even before then, you will commence battle training under the commanders who brought you here, who in turn will answer to me.' He walked down the steps to join his father, who had been standing to one side.

Wilfrid grinned at him. 'You enjoyed that, didn't you?'

'Born to lead, Father — born to lead.'

'Well, just remember, when Geoffrey finally gets here with the rest of the army, he will have been the one who recruited them. They will naturally answer to him. By all means amuse yourself with this lot from the de Clare entourage, but be prepared to see them absorbed into the main army in due course. You must then fall back into your rightful place at the head of the "Royal Guard", as I gather you have chosen to call it. You are fortunate that the previous guard was so disorganised and lacking in leadership, leaving the role open for you.'

'Or perhaps I displayed greater natural leadership,' Thomas smirked.

His father's face clouded over. 'There is more to leadership than yelling orders, Thomas. You must also possess the strength and determination to drive the men on over the corpses of their comrades who have fallen ahead of them. You must be prepared to walk slowly through your wounded after the battle, putting a merciful end to those who plead for it.'

Thomas went a little pale as he nodded. 'I was on Crusade, remember. I have seen and done all those things.'

'And do you wish to see and do them again?'

'No, not really.'

'Then do not boast of your leadership skills. Leave those sickening tasks to Geoffrey. Now, have you enough accommodation for these warriors of yours?'

'There are several barrack blocks around the main keep, plus a stables in which some of the mounted men may sleep alongside their horses.'

'I remember those well enough. Your sister was conceived in one of them. Or was she? I forget now.'

'What of the men that Geoffrey will be bringing in?' asked Thomas.

'A very apt question. I'll ask the Chamberlain to scour the town for billets for them. It will not be easy, and the sooner they ride out again the better. But they must at some point be blended with those who are here already, in order to make one cohesive army with recognised commanders. Use the ones who brought them from Tonbridge and Hertford as your seconds in command, and leave it to them to organise the ranks beneath them. It is better for men that they fight alongside, and under, men they know.'

'Until they have to see them fall in combat, that is,' Thomas muttered uneasily.

'Your time on Crusade was clearly not entirely spent in gambling and lusting after women,' his father replied sadly.

Ten days later, Geoffrey arrived with another thousand men. Westminster degenerated into a noisy chaos that reminded Wilfrid of the day he had arrived with the entire Wessex Fyrd in a show of strength for Earl Harold Godwinson. Day after day, both keeps rang with the sound of sword on shield and vibrated with the thuds of lances on targets. Wilfrid left detailed training to Geoffrey and Thomas, secure in the knowledge that they would be so preoccupied with keeping such large numbers of men in order that they would have no time for bickering between themselves.

They met each evening in Wilfrid's private chamber on the ground floor of the main palace to discuss how the training was going, and to make provisional plans for the allocation of men into fighting wings. It was from there that Wilfrid was summoned urgently by an usher sent by King Henry.

'We are being invaded,' Henry advised Wilfrid just as he walked through the door.

'Duke Robert?' Wilfrid enquired.

Henry nodded. 'Sails have been spotted off the south coast at Pevensey.'

'Not Portsmouth, as Thomas predicted?'

'No. It seems that my brother has a sense of history. Our father landed somewhere around there, did he not?'

'Indeed he did, sire, and I remember, as a young man, watching the sails appearing over the horizon as if they would never cease. How large is Robert's force?'

'Not as large as we expected, apparently. The best estimate is twenty large vessels.'

'Two thousand men and horses, then. How do you propose that we proceed?'

'You're the soldier, Wilfrid. What do you advise?'

'Clearly a show of defensive force. I was born in a village just north of Pevensey, and I know the lie of the land, so it might be best if I accompany you.'

'You think I should go in person?'

'It's traditional, sire. And, if they want to parley, you are there in person to agree the terms.'

Henry snorted. 'Tell me, Wilfrid, from the depth of your military experience, did you ever know of a man with two thousand soldiers behind him who wanted to parley?'

'How experienced is your brother in warfare?' Wilfrid enquired.

'More than me, obviously. He was on Crusade also, remember.'

'From what I heard, his horse displayed more leadership than he did. However, at this stage we must take him seriously.'

'How many men do you have ready?'

'A thousand — perhaps two.'

'That is less than Robert would seem to have.'

'Yes, but I have the advantage of a detailed knowledge of the terrain. Added to which, I believe I may be able to recruit more once we arrive there. If it suits Your Majesty, we can leave at first light tomorrow.'

A cockerel was crowing somewhere as Wilfrid climbed gingerly onto the rear of a baggage wagon to address the sleepy-looking men at arms ranged across the inner keep.

'For most of your lives, most of you have fought only straw targets, or thrust blunted swords and lances at your comrades in arms. The time has now come to test the skills you have been perfecting on real soldiers fighting for a real enemy. We proceed south-west of here, to the Sussex coast, to repel a moderate invasion force from Normandy. Some of you may be old enough, like me, to remember a previous force that came from Normandy, on the day that Duke William became King of England. It is time to show that the loss we suffered then was due solely to lack of numbers. Each of your commanders has been given his orders, and we are well supplied. We should be there in three days or so, and I will address you again when we are. Now, move out and let's get on with it.'

Henry had been listening from the doorway to his suite of rooms in the Palace, and as the 'hurrah' went up from the men, he walked out to his waiting horse. Its bridle was being held by Thomas, surrounded by a dozen men selected from the Royal Guard to accompany their king to the confrontation with his brother Robert. Wilfrid walked across the keep to his own waiting horse, slipped the groom a few coins and climbed into the saddle to take his place to the left of the king, with Thomas to Henry's right. As they trotted gently across the moat and down between the rows of houses in which palace servants were accommodated, the conversation was all about the threat to the nation.

'How soon before the rest of the army can join us?' Henry enquired.

'A matter of days only, sire,' Wilfrid reassured him. 'Geoffrey wishes to complete their training and allocate leadership roles to their best men, then he is instructed to ride out behind us. He should be with us before we need to engage the enemy.'

'And I have left sufficient men behind to guard the palace in your absence, sire,' Thomas added. 'It's as well that there was no royal family to leave behind.'

'There may be before much longer,' Henry grinned. 'We recently received an emissary from Scotland, offering me the hand of the Princess Matilda. It would be a very tactical opportunity to put a stop to those irritating raids across our northern borders, and the lady herself is said to be not without beauty.'

'No more news of the proposed marriage alliance with Blois?' Thomas enquired as casually as he could.

'I think we may safely conclude that those proposals have been overtaken by the appearance of Norman sails on our horizon,' Wilfrid commented as they finally reached open country. They rode at a slow pace, since every mile took them further ahead of their army, most of whom were trudging through light mud created by the first of the autumn rains. They camped for two nights on riverbanks, and each night the main army caught up with them in order to share the basic provisions that had been loaded into the wagons by the palace cooks.

On the third day, in the late afternoon, Wilfrid pointed down the track that led south from the Winchester road towards the distant sea. From the ridge on which they sat, Norman sails could be seen bobbing lightly up and down on a receding tide, and Wilfrid shared his thoughts with the other two.

'Your father came inland immediately and set up camp on the foreshore, sire. But Robert seems content to remain out at sea.'

'His soldiers will not be pleased,' said Thomas. 'If they are experiencing what we went through on the Black Sea on our second Crusade expedition, there'll be vomiting over the sides, and will not be fit for battle when they do come ashore.'

'*If* they come ashore,' Wilfrid responded thoughtfully. 'Either your brother Robert is an even worse strategist than I imagined, sire, or the fleet we can see is a diversion from their main force. They should have established their landfall bridgehead long before now, just as your father did. It will be much easier for us to take them on while they are tumbling out of their vessels onto the shingle.'

'Portsmouth!' Thomas cut in. 'I believed all along that the party that came to Westminster, claiming to be from Blois, were really from Normandy, and that their real objective was to spy out the land around Portsmouth. It's a much larger harbour for their vessels, and they could disembark ten thousand men in less than two hours.'

'Let's hope they don't *have* ten thousand men,' Wilfrid muttered, 'but you may be right. While we sit and watch half their total force bobbing up and down in front of Pevensey, the other half could be disembarking at Portsmouth and attacking us from the west.'

'Do you wish me to ride west and investigate, Father?' Thomas offered eagerly.

Wilfrid shook his head. 'That would divide our already diminished force. Better to wait until Geoffrey arrives with the rest of our army. Then he can be sent to investigate, and perhaps stand against them.'

'Geoffrey again,' Thomas muttered. 'So what do you propose that *we* do, in the meantime?'

'Give the impression that we've fallen for their ruse,' Wilfrid suggested. 'Take the men we have down towards Pevensey, and pick up a few more in Sandlake while we're about it. While we're all sitting watching each other, Geoffrey can slip behind us and march on to Portsmouth.'

'Why does the name "Sandlake" sound familiar?' Thomas enquired.

'It's where I was born, Thomas. I put together one fyrd thirty or so years ago down there, and now I intend to recruit another.'

As the sun began to set, Wilfrid guided their army down the track as far as Powdermill Lake, two miles or so above the coastline. There was enough open ground for the men to pitch the tents they had brought from London, and ample fishing in the lake itself, both to provide fresh food and to occupy the restless men. As he stood at the side of the Powdermill track that led down to Sandlake, breathing in the mouth-watering smell of fish cooking on the open fires behind him, Wilfrid allowed his memories to come flooding back. When Thomas silently slipped to his side, he was in the mood for reminiscence.

'Thirty something years ago, I was on the run from Thegn Leofric. I believed I had killed his older son, Uncle Selwyn's brother. I hid up here, living on fish, and here I was found by one of Earl Harold's captains. It was that meeting that led me into the earl's service, and that was how I came to recruit men from that village below us, and fight Duke William on the ridge they now call Senlac. When he became king, William was planning to build a mighty church where the thegn's house once stood — we might take a look at it tomorrow.'

'Do you regret joining the losing side?' Thomas enquired tactlessly.

'No — and neither should you, since it was what led to my meeting your mother.'

'I'm not sure it's all that healthy to be thinking back to the past the way you've being doing lately.'

'Well, that's unfortunate,' Wilfrid replied, 'because tomorrow you'll be going back into the past with me.'

The next morning, they trotted side by side down the Powdermill track. Thomas listened politely as Wilfrid pointed out various scenes from his childhood, and recounted stories that meant nothing to his son, other than to reinforce the point that his father had led an eventful life, and that it was perhaps the right time for him to be hanging up his armour and sword belt.

A weathered old mill came into sight, and Wilfrid was halfway through describing how it worked — as if Thomas cared — and how he'd developed his muscles heaving sacks of grain onto the bottom stone. Then he broke off as a man's sweating face appeared through the opening in the platform, breathing hard as his double chins wobbled with the effort. Wilfrid leapt from his horse and rushed as fast as his ageing limbs permitted towards the mill, calling out as he did so.

'Deman, you old bastard! Is that really you?'

'The last man who called me a bastard finished up looking fer 'is teeth up 'is arse,' the fat old man replied threateningly. 'An' who are *you*, with yer fancy armour an' yer big 'orse? Come ter recruit men ter fight the French, 'ave yer? Well, leave — me fightin' days is over!'

'Deman,' Wilfrid persisted, 'don't you recognise me? It's Will Riveracre!'

'Who?' Thomas and Deman replied in unison. The old name was unfamiliar to the son, but then Deman Flesher seemed to remember something.

'I were told yer'd left 'ere never ter come back. Good riddance an' all. While yer was 'ere, all yer did was get village folk killed, then yer took up with them French.'

'Deman and I used to be enemies in our youth,' Wilfrid explained to a bemused Thomas, 'and it looks as if things haven't changed much around here.' Then he looked back up at the corpulent figure with the red face hanging off the mill platform. 'You don't look much like a fighting man anymore,' he smiled at Deman. 'Does the village still have a fyrd?'

'Yeah, except it's called the "Village Watch" these days, an' me son Oswyn's in charge of it. I suppose them sails out ter sea means more invaders?'

'I'm afraid so, and the king is camped up by Powdermill Lake, looking for more recruits for his army.'

Deman tutted loudly, squatted down and jumped off the platform. Then he waved his hand for the two visitors to accompany him, and led them to a hut in the second row back from the track. He called out as he approached the entrance.

'Oswyn! 'Ere's an' old troublemaker come ter borrer yer Watch. They remember 'im as an 'ero around these parts, but 'e's still the braggin' old fartbag that 'e always was.'

A younger version of Deman poked his head from the hut entrance. He looked just like his father, and had obviously acquired his manners as well.

'So who *are* yer, exactly?'

'Will Riveracre.'

'*The* Will Riveracre? But 'e's dead, they reckon.'

'Then I must be his ghost,' Wilfrid chuckled. 'Either way, I need your men to join the king's army up the road there.'

'Yer jokin', surely?' Oswyn replied. 'Yer the bloke what saved the village from the Norman bastard? An' now yer wants *me* ter join yer in doin' it again?'

'Not me.' Wilfrid gestured towards the man beside him. 'My son Thomas, who commands the Royal Guard.'

'The bloody Riveracres always *did* reckon they was summat special,' Deman grumbled as he stood back slightly. 'This bastard even wanted ter marry yer old mam afore she chose me instead.'

'How is Annis?' Wilfrid enquired politely.

Deman shook his head. 'Gone, a few months back. The fever took 'er, an' she's buried next ter yer own mam an' dad.'

'When d'yer want the men?' Oswyn asked.

Wilfrid smiled back at him encouragingly. 'Yesterday. How many have you got?'

'Forty or so, at a pinch. Up the road, yer say?'

'Yes — by Powdermill Lake.'

'Yer'll 'ave 'em afore the sun's at its 'ighest,' Oswyn promised him.

Wilfrid gave him his profuse thanks before turning back to Deman. 'I don't suppose you'll be joining them, my friend, but it was nice exchanging the usual pleasantries with you.'

'Bloody Riveracres,' Deman grinned reluctantly as he held out his hand. 'Gimme yer 'and, afore yer gets it cut off by forriners.'

'Was that fat oaf really once a warrior?' Thomas asked disbelievingly as they rode back up the track towards the lake.

Wilfrid nodded. 'Hard to believe, I know, but he was once the only man in the village who could flatten me — if he got a hold of me, that is. He was always a bit slow, but he once commanded the local "fyrd", as we called it then, and he cut off more Norman heads on Senlac Ridge than anyone else from Sandlake.'

'He obviously had a high opinion of you,' Thomas replied sarcastically.

'Our relationship was a lot like yours and Geoffrey's. Talking of whom, let's hope he doesn't keep us waiting too long.'

Three days later, Wilfrid and Thomas met Geoffrey and the rest of the army at the junction of the main Pevensey track with the Winchester road. Geoffrey was in an ebullient mood and advised Wilfrid that a rousing cheer had gone up from the ranks when they had first caught sight of the Norman sails out to sea.

'They can't wait to get stuck into them,' he enthused.

'Well, they'll have to wait,' Wilfrid cautioned him. 'It seems likely that the small force out there is simply intended to divert our attention from their main army, which we believe is heading for Portsmouth, and may well be there already. I'll come with you to see what, if anything, is happening further west, while Thomas can go back down to the king and supervise his forces.'

Thomas tutted, then turned round and shouted the order for his men to move on down the track towards the sea.

'You'll at least remain in the king's eye,' Wilfrid consoled him. 'In my experience, when a military leader experiences a victory, he tends to associate it with, and reward, those who were closest to him physically during the encounter. As for Geoffrey, it'll be a case of "out of sight, out of mind". Tell King Henry that I'll ride back quickly once I learn how the land lies in Portsmouth.'

It was not quite daylight, three days later, when Wilfrid commanded all the men to rouse from their tents, minus their armour so as not to cause any flashes of light when the sun rose over the village of Portsmouth. They stood there in a largely silent mass, shoulder to shoulder, until first light, then Wilfrid ordered them to lie flat on their faces. They were on the only piece of rising land to be found on this flat coastal plain, and below them the first things to come into sight were the white sails of the enemy vessels that lay in the wide harbour. Between the royal ranks and the enemy there lay some sort of island which could only be crossed by a narrow bridge, on which the Normans had stationed a handful of heavily armed men.

There was not much sign of action on the decks of the ships. Wilfrid guessed that the invaders had already sacked the small town, and were now sleeping it off among the sparsely spread huts along the foreshore and the narrow street behind it.

'What do you think?' Geoffrey enquired as he lay next to Wilfrid, squinting his eyes against the rising sun. The blinding effect of the strong orange glow from the east gave Wilfrid an idea.

'How many battle pennants did you bring?'

'More than we needed, I suspect. We have just over a thousand men, barring any early desertions, and some fool packed enough pennants for over twice that number. Why do you need to know?'

'Get the men to plant the pennants in the ground every hundred yards or so across the rise here, to give the impression that we have more men than we actually do. Then get six or so men to stand around the pennants looking impatient for action. The rest of the men are to remain flat on the ground in turns, then get up and walk around, creating the impression of a busy camp.'

'What do you intend to happen?'

'I want that lot down below to think they're outnumbered, then head off towards London on the low ground. Then you follow behind them, and drive them straight onto the king's forces further east. I'll be riding back hard to prepare them.'

An hour later there was movement in the town, as men who had been ferried off the ships in the harbour could be seen moving in and out of the buildings on the waterfront. Columns of men slowly took up positions, and on a shouted command in French that was audible even up the hill, they marched off eastwards in disciplined columns. Wilfrid was just congratulating himself on his battlefield strategy when he noticed an enemy ship under full sail heading into the harbour from the open ocean. He smiled and called Geoffrey over to his side.

'Robert of Normandy is either a better strategist than I gave him credit for, or he is well advised by others. My guess is that they're trying to tempt us out into the open on the flat ground behind them, and that a second force will then be brought ashore to form a pincer so that we can be attacked from both sides. Well, two can play at that game. Divide your force in two, and leave half with me.'

Wilfrid's foresighted strategy was rewarded two hours later, when ten more vessels sailed swiftly into the harbour and discharged roughly a thousand men onto the waterfront. They formed up in a considerable hurry and marched off eastwards, several miles behind the first wave of Normans that had set off in an easterly direction, followed by Geoffrey's men. Wilfrid gave a triumphant grin and ordered his men down the slope after them.

There were now four armed contingents marching east. First came the original Norman force, followed a mile behind by Geoffrey and half his army. Then came the pursuing second wave of Normans who had just come ashore, and no doubt believed that they were about to attack the English forces two miles ahead of them in the rear once their first wave stopped and turned to engage the enemy. They were in fact so assured that this stratagem would work that no-one thought to look behind as Wilfrid's platoons narrowed the distance between them.

Wilfrid spotted the herald positioned on the rock to the seaward of the fields they were plodding through, and could just make out the fact that the man was yelling something at the top of his voice before he placed a horn to his lips and gave a series of blasts that was some sort of signal. There appeared to have been a change of plan, because the second cohort of Normans stopped suddenly and turned to face Wilfrid's advancing force with a line of menacing spears and shouts that were unintelligible to the English, but which Wilfrid translated in his head as invitations to advance to their deaths.

He spurred his mount forward and rode swiftly past the ends of the ranks that were confronting each other until he reached the next standoff. Geoffrey's force had the superior numbers, and while five ranks faced forward to where the forward Normans were glowering at them, five other ranks had turned and were showing the enemy behind them a defensive shield wall bristling with spears and lances. The second wave of Normans were effectively surrounded, and they had been caught in their own trap.

Wilfrid rode over to where a forest of Norman battle pennants betrayed the presence of Duke Robert and his military advisers. He pulled hard on the reins when he spotted the diminutive form of Duke Robert himself, mounted on a massive destrier. Then he nudged his mount towards the duke.

'A nice tactic!' Wilfrid shouted. 'So nice that we decided to copy it.'

'Where is my brother Henry?' Robert demanded.

'Further east, admiring the small fleet you sent as a decoy. Your soldiers must be heartily seasick after all this time.'

'I wish to speak to Henry,' Robert insisted.

Wilfrid gave him a mock bow. 'As a family man myself, who am I to stand in the way of such a reunion? Follow me and I will lead you to him. I'll ride alone, if you undertake to do the same.'

XXV

'You're an underhanded, treacherous stealer of thrones!' Robert yelled accusingly across the few feet of grass that separated the two brothers.

'And you're *still* a short-arse!' Henry retorted.

'You'd probably steal my horse from under me!'

Up to three thousand men could hear this irate exchange between the remaining sons of the once all-powerful ruler of Normandy and England. Those men at arms who spoke French were doubling up with laughter. Their English counterparts, while unable to understand what the two angry brothers were yelling at each other, could tell from the tones of their voices that it was far from brotherly. They were grinning as they took their lead from the French soldiers, relieved that the immediate threat of bloody slaughter seemed to have dissolved. Wilfrid decided that enough was enough, and attempted to steer the exchange back to a peace agenda.

'Sire,' he whispered to Henry, 'we have almost three thousand men on both sides of us, who came here expecting a battle. I for one don't care to be in the middle if fighting breaks out.'

Henry appeared taken aback for a moment, but at least he modified the tone of his voice as he glared across at Robert. 'You clearly came here intending to take my crown from me. Equally clearly that has failed, so what terms do you propose for your withdrawal?'

'Who said I was about to withdraw?' Robert demanded stubbornly.

'I did — just then,' Henry replied.

Robert appeared to think deeply before replying. 'How much is your kingdom worth to you? How much will you pay me to stay away forever?'

'What did you have in mind?'

'The former Saxon kings of England paid the Danes an annual sum to stay away — what say you that we revive that tradition?'

'A thousand marks a year?'

Robert laughed contemptuously. 'Is that all you value your country at? Five thousand.'

'Two thousand.'

'Pounds.'

'Agreed. Now, what about the marriage treaty? I assume that it's been abandoned, if it ever really existed, and you should know that I will probably be marrying into the royal house of Scotland.'

'But it didn't involve you, did it?' Robert reminded him. 'It was to do with a noblewoman from Blois and your new Treasurer — is your memory that short?'

'Stephen never formally agreed to my final terms. Do you carry his authority in your saddlebag?'

'It just so happens that I do,' Robert smirked. 'Our brother-in-law has taken himself back on Crusade, probably to escape our sister's nagging tongue, and he has left me to convey his consent to your last proposal. Rather over-generous on his part, I fear, but your Treasurer will be all the happier to know that his bride will be of royal blood, if perhaps from the wrong side of the marital bed.'

Wilfrid felt Thomas go rigid with horror as he stood alongside him in the press of men, and he seemed to be whispering a prayer as Robert continued.

'It seems that during one of his forays into Aquitaine, Stephen got his leg over a lady of the court there. The result was the Lady Emma, as she is called. Our sister loathes the very ground she walks on, and Stephen has been bullied by his wife into sacrificing her in the cause of ongoing peace between Blois and England. She is currently in Cherbourg, awaiting shipment like a consignment of fleeces. Once we agree this peace treaty today, she can be over here within the week.'

'No!' Thomas whispered, gripping his sword hilt.

Wilfrid hastened to place a firm hand over his arm. 'Leave it, Thomas,' he warned him hoarsely. 'There are other women, and there are too many witnesses.'

'There will never be another like Emma,' Thomas replied, on the verge of tears, 'and what of the child? Nobody has mentioned that she has a child — will that destroy the treaty?'

'I doubt it,' Wilfrid whispered back. 'For now, let's just listen.'

At that moment Henry looked behind him, and his eyes lit upon Wilfrid. 'Sir Wilfrid, do we have any clerks in our company?'

'You would not have thanked me to man your army with monks, sire, but I can read and write, as can my son here. What is it you require?'

'A peace treaty, drawn up before both armies leave the field. There appears to be an abbey of some sort in the distance there, and we may make use of its facilities. What is this place called?'

'Alton, sire,' came a voice from the ranks.

'Very well,' Henry replied, 'let us proceed to yon abbey and draw up " The Treaty of Alton". But there is another matter I must attend to first. Sir Wilfrid, who else led your men from Portsmouth?'

'Geoffrey de Faverches, sire. He took the more hazardous role of drawing off the Normans from their intended ambush.'

'I thought that might have been the case. Geoffrey de Faverches, come forward!'

There was a ripple of chainmail as the English ranks parted in the centre, and Geoffrey stepped forward.

'Kneel!' Henry commanded, as he drew his sword. Geoffrey knelt as commanded, and Wilfrid heard another suppressed groan from Thomas.

'Kneel, Geoffrey de Faverches, and rise *Sir* Geoffrey de Faverches.'

'Don't give me any nonsense about "I'll get over it in due course",' Thomas slurred, and his father tactfully removed the wine goblet from his hand as they stood on the fringes of the English camp at Powdermill Lake. 'And to twist the knife in further, the bastard wants me to be the one to convey her with great ceremony into Winchester, where she is to be married to some smelly old man!'

'A brief word of advice from a father who has seen a little of life, and wants his son to live to see it also,' Wilfrid muttered. 'Do not refer to the king as a bastard, do not drink any more wine this evening, and do not believe that the Lady Emma is the only woman in the world.'

'She's the only one who has my child in her keeping,' Thomas choked. 'I suppose there's always the hope that either the Treasurer will reject her when he learns that she is soiled goods, or that he will offer up the child for someone like me to care for.'

'That reminds me,' Wilfrid said by way of diversion, 'once we return from Winchester, we must lose no time in riding home. Geoffrey will be there well ahead of us, bearing news that we have survived, but he will also alert your mother to the fact that we are delaying our own return.'

'I believe that you're more scared of Mother than you are of Robert of Normandy,' Thomas managed with a weak smile.

'Indeed I am,' Wilfrid replied with a smile of his own, relieved that the crisis appeared to be over, 'and so should you be, if you aren't already. Also your sister, to whom you promised a small niece of her own to look after, or so she advised me in confidence. She grows more clucky by the day in that orphanage of hers, and any man who manages to win her hand may well find himself the father of more children than he ever dreamed of.'

'I just hope I get to be the father of little Elinor,' Thomas muttered darkly.

'We leave at first light, with half a dozen of your Royal Guard to escort the Lady Emma to Winchester, or so I'm told.'

'Yes — she should have set sail yesterday, after Duke Robert sailed back across to Cherbourg to give them the so-called good news. The newly knighted *Sir* Geoffrey will celebrate his title by taking the rest of the men back to London, from where they can disperse. I believe that King Henry plans to release the de Clares with a final kick up the arse by way of heavy monetary penalties that will reimburse him the first year's bribe to his brother to stay out of England.'

'If we are to leave at first light, we should get some sleep.'

'You're probably right. Can I have my wine goblet back?'

'Have you ever ridden at first light with a hangover?'

'No.'

'A little more fatherly advice. Don't. The wine goblet goes back to the tent with me.'

XXVI

On the morning of the ninth day after the battle that never actually occurred, father and son were back in Portsmouth, this time on the waterfront. They watched the square-rigged knarr flying the emblem of Blois on its white sails, which it lowered before switching to oar power for the final half mile or so. As it ground alongside the quay, harbour hands raced to secure the ropes thrown from its side by liveried deckhands. Once the planking had been laid in place, the passengers disembarked in order to mount the horses that the English reception party had brought with them for the long day's ride to Winchester.

'Leave the official welcome to me,' Wilfrid instructed Thomas, who was only too happy to oblige as he looked sadly at the group of ladies with their attendants who were now standing on the quayside. To his utter amazement, he saw his father bowing politely to an elegant lady with long fair hair, and offering her his hand as the prize mare from the royal stables at Winchester was brought to her side. Thomas was about to rush down and advise his father that he had selected the wrong woman, but some instinct made him stop briefly. He then trotted his horse down to the assembling company.

'I believe you've met my son, Sir Thomas Walsingham?' Wilfrid oozed.

The lady with the fair hair smiled down at him from her horse. 'Indeed I have, and if he would care to dismount and seek out the Lady Melusine, who is one of the ladies behind me, she has a valuable package for him.'

Utterly bemused, but with hope growing stronger in his heart and churning stomach, Thomas moved down the line until he saw Emma. There was a huge loving smile on her face, a tear starting in one eye, and a carefully wrapped bundle in her arms.

'I am the Lady Melusine,' she advised him in a voice that was almost a sob. 'I have this precious bundle for delivery to your orphanage, but you must allow my attendant Armand to handle her. This is Armand by my side, and he is her physician, well accustomed to babies. Elinor is barely a year old, and requires care in her handling.'

Thomas fought back the tears as he dismounted, and nodded politely to the tall handsome courtier by her side, whose fresh face was glowing with pride. He appeared to be no older than thirty, and Thomas experienced a pang of jealous doubt as he wondered whether the man might be more to Emma than simply their daughter's physician. It fell silent for a moment, until Emma smiled lovingly again, this time at the bundle in her arms, and held her out towards Thomas.

'I must mount a horse, it seems. Would you be so good as to take the child from me briefly while I do so? Armand will also need to climb into a stirrup.'

It was all Thomas could do to restrain himself from smothering his beautiful daughter with kisses. He couldn't prevent the tears splashing down onto her delicate face with the big dark eyes that stared up at him quizzically. He handed the child back to Armand, and remounted. Once all the company was assembled, Wilfrid gave the command, and they moved off at a sedate pace up the gentle slope on their way to Winchester.

'How did you get away with it?' Thomas breathlessly enquired of Emma between their passionate kisses. They were behind the screen that divided the kitchen from the scullery in Winchester Castle, their conversation masked by the noise from the Great Hall in which the betrothal celebrations were drawing to a close. King Henry was expected to slide under the table shortly, and no-one seemed to have noticed their absence.

'It was all too easy,' Emma explained. 'Once we reached Cherbourg, I enquired which of my ladies wished to pose as me and marry a rich English noble. Sir Herbert will be none the wiser, and will be more than pleased with his new bride. No-one in England other than yourself has ever seen me, the attendants were richly bribed, my father is likely to get himself killed in the Holy Land, and my stepmother couldn't wave me off fast enough as we left the chateau at Blois. That leaves you and I free to make our lives together, but you must learn to call me "Melusine".'

Thomas kissed her passionately again. She sighed and shuddered slightly, then pushed him gently away.

'That must wait another hour or so, but I have reserved a separate chamber for "the Lady Melusine" here at the castle. Come to me once everyone else is either vomiting or unconscious.'

'Will you marry me?' Thomas blurted nervously.

Emma smiled. 'I did not come all this way, and engage in such elaborate subterfuge, to marry anyone else. May we live on your estate? Where is it?'

'A place called Walsingham, obviously, hence my title. It is in Norfolk, perhaps over a week's ride from here. Is our daughter fit to travel that distance?'

'Of course,' Emma replied. 'But you must let Armand accompany us, since he is the most skilled child physician in the whole of Aquitaine. You have an orphanage on your estate, I believe? Perhaps Armand could be given work there?'

'Of course — anything you wish. Let's go and see if everyone is unconscious yet…'

Even the sun had come out to join them as the happy party stood on the grass slope outside the shrine, with Mother Magdalena's grave mound to one side, as Elston, in his ordained priest's robes, began to intone the Latin verses for the celebration of holy matrimony. Thomas's parents stood proudly at his side, and on the far side of 'the Lady Melusine' was Sir Geoffrey Faverches, who had gallantly offered to stand in for her father. Elston finally pronounced them man and wife — in English as well as in Latin — and the crowd closed round the happy couple to offer their congratulations.

Mother Grace waved her hand, and the small choir of orphans broke hesitantly into the old English folk song they had been practising for a week, while her small party of nuns and novices moved among the wedding guests offering wine and sweetmeats. Wilfrid and Joan stood holding hands at the edge of the company, having been the first to congratulate the bride and groom. Wilfrid broke the silence as he looked towards the doorway of the shrine, where a smiling couple stood with their arms draped around each other.

'I think we shall shortly be requiring our nephew's services once again,' he smiled. 'Tilly seems to have really taken to that baby physician that Emma — sorry, "Lady Melusine" — brought over with her, and I'd hazard a guess that Armand is interested in more than just the babies in her orphanage. Brace yourself for many more grandchildren.'

A NOTE TO THE READER

Dear Reader,

Thank you for taking the time to read this second novel in a series of seven that between them cover the twelfth century, a period during which England was transformed beyond recognition. I hope that it lived up to your expectations. Once again, the basic plot was written for me by the events that really happened in the aftermath of the arrival of the Normans into an England previously dominated by Saxon society.

The circumstances surrounding the allegedly accidental death of King William II — 'William Rufus' — during a hunt in the New Forest in 1100 have provided historians and historical novelists with a mystery to rival that of the disappearance of the royal princes in the Tower in 1483 or thereabouts. There are several suspects, and in this novel I chose one of them, based on the events of Rufus's reign.

Duke William of Normandy was no doubt as proud of having sired four sons as he was of having added England to his territorial portfolio. But this legacy brought nothing but conflict to all his territories, and England was no exception. Following the death of his second son Richard — ironically, as the result of an accident in the New Forest — there were three remaining sons, none of whom had any great regard for the others. Upon William's death his favoured Normandy was left to the oldest son Robert, known as 'Curthose' due to his lack of height. Given that one's image as a warrior in those days was measured by one's stature, it was hardly surprising that Robert sought to overcome this shortness by adopting a bellicose attitude towards his younger brothers. In particular he insisted that he should have inherited the whole of their father's lands, including England.

The one who *had* been bequeathed England was a dissolute man who was probably the least qualified of the three brothers to govern a kingdom. Mean-spirited and debauched, William Rufus had favourites who were probably unfit to be granted high office over the affairs of the realm. Chief among these was Ranulf Flambard, who was almost certainly Rufus's lover, and who bore the brunt of the blame for the financial demands made of the remainder of the nobility. He was also pivotal in driving a wedge between King and Church that was financial in origin, since Rufus needed a regular and substantial flow of funds, and claimed the income of the Church during a lengthy period in which he steadfastly declined to appoint new bishops and archbishops on the deaths of their predecessors.

But Rufus's claim to England was hotly disputed by his older brother Robert, who was constantly plotting invasion, despite being distracted by the call of the Pope to embark on the Crusades to reclaim the Holy Land for Christianity. He unwisely financed his crusade ambitions by leasing Normandy to Rufus during his absence, and accompanying Robert on crusade was his brother-in-law Stephen of Blois, who had married William the Conqueror's daughter Adela.

The suggestion that Stephen of Blois had an illegitimate daughter, Emma, who married Henry I's Treasurer Herbert of Winchester, is supported by fourteenth-century records, but disputed by later historians. But it was all the excuse I needed to provide a love interest for Thomas Walsingham, and to give the story an added twist with the suggestion that she changed places with a woman from the Court of Aquitaine.

The death of William Rufus was, by any reckoning, fortuitous for his younger brother Henry, known as 'Beauclerc' because of his early preference for learning rather than warfare. So fortuitous, in fact, that some historians have suggested that either Henry killed Rufus himself, or arranged his death at the hands of Walter Tyrrell, and one could easily imagine — as I did for the purposes of this novel — that Henry was anxious to clear his name of that accusation when he became king, and others began to contest his right to rule England.

Chief among these was his older brother Robert, who in 1101 made one final attempt to become King of England by invading via Portsmouth. He was forced to surrender after serious tactical blunders that are imagined towards the end of the novel. The resulting Treaty of Alton held good for only four years, until Henry repaid the compliment and successfully invaded Robert's lands in Normandy.

But the next dynastic struggle in the aftermath of England's conquest from across the Channel was not long in coming. Henry I of England died in 1135, unleashing bitter warfare between the two cousins Matilda and Stephen that form the background to the next novel in this series, *An Uncivil War.*

As ever, I look forward to receiving feedback from you in the form of a review on **Amazon** or **Goodreads**. Or, of course, you can try the more personal approach on my website, and my Facebook page: **DavidFieldAuthor**.

Happy reading!

David

davidfieldauthor.com

Sapere Books is an exciting new publisher of brilliant fiction and popular history.

To find out more about our latest releases and our monthly bargain books visit our website:
saperebooks.com

Made in the USA
Las Vegas, NV
28 April 2024

89255446R00125